An Adolescent's Soul Grows in the North Woods

Robert C. Jones

Robert C. Jones

A publication of

Eber & Wein Publishing

Pennsylvania

An Adolescent's Soul Grows in the North Woods

Library of Congress
Cataloging in Publication Data

ISBN 978-1-60880-776-5

Proudly manufactured in the United States of America by

Eber & Wein Publishing

Pennsylvania

Dedicated to our three grandsons—Brandon, Joshua, Justin—who always enjoy a good story fictionalized or otherwise and to the Romeo District Library and Kezar branches of the Romeo District Library system.

Inspiration for the diver is credited to Janina Parrott Jacobs.

All references to names, dates, and places are accurate as researched by the author to the best of his ability. Parts of this story are fictional to enhance the narrative and to move the story forward.

This story takes place in the early 1960s, a time long before cell phones and with limited computer systems. The North Woods on the Big Lake is mostly still a pristine environment.

Contents

Chapter 1.
Introduction 1

Chapter 2.
Pacing Off a Piece of Property Together—The Shoe Does Fit 7

Chapter 3.
A New Contraption—Trouble Brewing 12

Chapter 4.
Bob Meets Janina's Younger Sister 19

Chapter 5.
Fishing on the Big Lake—Catch of the Day (maybe the season) 32

Chapter 6.
A Celebration—Isabella's Quinceañera 39

Chapter 7.
A Fire—Prominent Member of the Community Succumbs 50

Chapter 8.
The Community Unites: An Event at Persons Harbor
Craft Fair and a Wake 61

Chapter 9.
A Trip to Traverse to Save the Inn 72

Chapter 10.
Life's Lessons Learned Well—Bob's Soul to Keep in the North Woods 79

Addendum 94

Part II
Bob's Young Soul Continues to Grow in the North Woods 97

Chapter 1.

Introduction

The big lake sparkled like diamonds, boaters skimming across tranquil waters going out into the deepest part of the lake perhaps traversing the eighteen-mile length, perhaps across the three-mile wide width.

The yachting vessels were decked out, masts stretching, catching the early summer breeze, which was mildly yawning in today's tranquil mood; certainly a south wind, not a howler from the north.

A young adolescent emerged from a tan station wagon, his mother bending his ear with directives to mind his manners, say thank you, follow your uncle and aunt's instructions, and eat everything on your plate. And *"Please, please* help people whom you can help—even without being asked—especially that Dan guy at the market and your friend Pip at the Marina.

"Help your aunt with her chores if she asks. Oh, you know your paper route is covered for the next two weeks; your dad can do without you for two weeks. Maybe your baseball team needs you, but you'll only miss two games with the break in the season. And Scout camp doesn't begin until later in the summer.

"Oh, and stay clean. You and those Bond boys. My, my. Last summer, it was all I could do to get grease and the smell of diesel fuel out of your clothes.

"I know Doctor Bond passed away last summer, but his grand-children probably will be coming up.

"One last comment from your mom—have fun!"

His aunt and uncle appeared on the back porch of the large Italianate home often referred to by neighbors, friends, and business associates as The Big House.

His aunt was first to greet Nephew, hugging him, holding him close. "Welcome, Bob. You're lookin' all grown up. It's been since Christmas since we saw you. My what six months growth can accomplish."

His uncle behind his aunt took the pipe out of his mouth and welcomed him: "I'll be a monkey's uncle, Nephew, er Bob; you're gettin' as tall as those pine trees in the Allward Forest.

"Get out the ice cream, deary. Chocolate sundaes on the porch in the moonlight—just the violin sounds of the chirpin' crickets makin' beautiful music."

Aunty blurted: "Those crickets are just fish bait, dear Uncle. Won't you come in and sit a spell, mom—enjoy a meal?"

"No thanks. I've got to get back to manage the remaining herd."

Her last words to Bob: "Now you mind your P's and Q's, son."

Uncle came back to say: "There are many theories about those letters—pints and quarts, watch what you drink, a sailor's peacoat and a queue, a long plait of hair, or maybe early in our history telling those young printers to be careful about not pressing the letter Q when you mean P and vice-versa," Uncle now out of breath.

Mom looked at Uncle and wrinkled her brow, glad he was finished with his long-winded explanation.

Aunty gave Uncle her elbow in the rib—a physical sign to cool it.

Uncle only smiled, relocated his pipe to his lips, took a drag, and uttered, "Dang flame went out. They don't make meerschaums like they used to."

Mom waved as she drove away. Bob brought his grip into The Big House. He knew he would have his choice of rooms upstairs. After seven previous years coming up, he knew the S.O.P. his uncle would tell him from time to time relating to a number of matters both domestic and business—standard operating procedure.

This first night would set the agenda for the visit.

The crickets were chirping—maybe wanting a part of Aunty's famous baked chicken, a side of mixed vegetables, and special honey-soaked biscuits with a dollop of jampot preserve slathered on top.

For dessert Aunty's special peach cobbler. The ice cream sundaes would wait to be part of the late evening "snacking"—Uncle's term until the following evening.

"Now get some rest, Nephew. I have some work for you to do tomorrow. I'll get the full measure of your effort then. My saying for the evening is *if the shoe fits wear it.*" Uncle smiled to himself at this, he thought, bit of sage advice.

Bob selected the upstairs front bedroom again this summer.

The theme was definitely nautical. He always wondered how the ship fit into the glass bottle, a piece high up on the mantel. There didn't seem to be any seams in the glass. He only concluded there must have been a very patient person who used tweezers to inject the parts into the bottle piece by piece.

Other items included flags used by sailors to denote various nautical terms and emergencies generally found onboard a yacht.

Then there was the wooden replica of the USS Constitution also placed on the mantel. It hadn't been dusted in quite a while. Aunty had it given to her by her grandmother. She said this was an heirloom to be kept in the family.

At each end of the huge rectangular room was a rattan chair, which, to Bobby, was quite uncomfortable to sit on.

On the large king-size bed were pillows of all shapes and sizes. Aunty called these accent pieces.

The large billowy down bedspread expressed itself with a variety of boats, ships, and yachts painted onto the spread.

Bobby put his clothes in the large armoire fashioned from mahogany and cherrywood. This large piece of furniture swallowed up his two-week allotment in his grip. He would choose only two drawers from many to hide his wares.

Uncle informed him the upstairs bathroom was still not finished. He had not found another construction worker after Barny's untimely death last season.

"Use the pee pot if you have to go. I wouldn't want you stumbling down the stairs at night as the only usable bathroom was on the first floor. Keep your vitals under wrap and key if at all possible—*capiche*?

Nephew prayed, then let his mind wander as he snuggled deeper and deeper under the covers. What did Uncle mean "if the shoe fits wear it?" Let these adventures begin again this summer. *Ahoy, matey!* Here we go again.

Chapter 2.

Pacing Off a Piece of Property Together—
The Shoe Does Fit

Uncle stopped the truck a mile up the road from the Big House. He was very quiet at breakfast, allowing Aunty to take charge fueling Nephew for the day's activities.

Nephew broke the silence as both retreated from the truck and walked to the edge of a culvert. Uncle waved his hands, pointing out a panoramic view of acreage with a large cherry orchard in the back of the property.

"Now here's where your feet are gonna work to parcel off this piece of land. Last night Aunty measured your shoe size. Size twelve. Exactly a foot long. Okay, tenderfoot, I want you to walk in as straight a line as possible up this hill four hundred feet to the back of the property. Take this stake. Stick it in the ground. Then go due east to your right, young man, three hundred feet. Put the second stake in the ground. Then come down back this way. Do the same completing the process. *Capiche?*"

"So we're here to measure off some new property you just bought," Nephew responded casually.

"Yes, and that's not all I've got to tell you. We're building a new home on this site. The old Big House is too much for us to keep up anymore . . . too many repairs have to be made. Its plumbing is old, too many cracks in the plaster, in need of a new

roof . . . I could go on and on. Aunty picked out the design for the new home. She wanted a clear view of the Big Lake. It'll be smaller, but new and much more manageable.

"Oh, and we're sellin' the cabins. Too much work and just barely breakin' even. The big money for us is at Deep Water Point, sellin' those lots I purchased around the point.

"You know the saying 'it's hard to hit a moving target.' Time to move ahead. More people want to move up here from down-state."

With this last comment he motioned to Bob, "Be careful to measure accurately, young man. You can count to four hundred, can't you?

"And oh, see that shed up yonder just this side of the orchard. Tell me when you return if it's on our property."

Nephew sized up his job, thankful to be considered useful in this endeavor. He hoped this would be the first of many such experiences to take place on this visit.

"I gotcha, Uncle. Thanks for counting on me." With that he took the stakes and proceeded up the hill one foot at a time careful to mark every foot as directed.

This job finished, Nephew met Uncle at the bottom of the hill. "Say, I want to know if that shed up yonder is on our property?" inquired Uncle, now face to face with Nephew.

"It seems to be. It's just inside the lot line I measured off. It certainly is run down and dumpy lookin'—a shack to be sure. The front door has a lock on it, but it appears broken. I didn't go up to it—didn't touch anything.

"There was a window on the side—all muddied up though." Nephew was getting up a full head of steam. "Maybe it has tools in it for fruit pickers—maybe just junk now though."

"Okay, okay thanks for the info. We'll come back tomorrow and take a look. Meanwhile I've got to get these specs over to the real estate office saying we staked our claim, get it notarized, tell the builders about it. They're gonna begin digging the foundation in a couple of weeks. Plenty to do, Nephew.

"I'll say you put your best foot forward today, young man. Your man-sized twelve shoe certainly fit the bill and did the deed. Finished in fine fashion—nose to the grindstone, sonny, er, Bob.

"Tomorrow we'll take a look inside that monstrosity of a shed like a couple of treasure hunters—don't know what we'll find."

Uncle reached over, hugged Nephew, stepped back, lit his pipe, took a few draws, and smiled up at the panoramic landscape. "A dream come true here, your aunty and me. New home and all. The future is here today. Look at that lake."

He turned to survey the other panoramic view. "Crystal clear water. Cold as a freezer keeping meat fresh. Blue as an azure sky—many shades of blue I might add.

"They say in all the journals keeping records of the most beautiful lakes in the world our Big Lake here is the eighth wonder of the world.

"Yes sir we'll come back tomorrow, look in that shed. Just some old rusty tools in there, I reckon. Come on, Bob, Aunty is waiting. Pot pie tonight. Bread pudding for dessert. A sundae later on the porch."

Both jumped into the truck. Uncle was heard humming "She'll be comin' 'round the mountain when she comes . . ."

"Tomorrow," he remarked, "we'll shed some light on that shed."

Yes, tomorrow is another day in the life of Bob and his uncle in the North Woods.

Chapter 3.

A New Contraption—Trouble Brewing

The rusty bolt lock stayed firm. "Hit it again with all your might, Nephew," said Uncle, now getting restless after eight or nine bangs on the mechanism to no avail. "We might have to bust a window and knock the frame out to get into this run-down shack." Just then *snap*, off it fell, success. Inside the smell was putrefying. Uncle thought a dead rat or two had found its way inside.

The two visitors focused their attention on the contents. There were shovels, pick axes, spades, and an old riding mower in the far corner. Burlap bags were everywhere. In the other corner lay a large toboggan along with several pairs of ice skates. But now the smell overcame Bob and his uncle, and they backed out. The opened door let this smell bolt out into the open air.

"Rats, where are the stinking rats?" said Uncle, peeking his head back into the building. It was then he noticed a strange looking contraption in the back of the shed, a circular metal band that fit around another object. Attached to this band was a motor with a switches on it—on, off, degree of speed, degree of vibration—all indicated on a metal plate.

"What have we found?" Nephew spoke up eager to touch the device and examine it from all sides. "Careful, tread slowly. You don't know if this machine has any live wires or parts that may start up if you touch it." Both stopped short. They took in this

strangely-shaped object, but it was left to the imagination as to exactly its purpose.

"Well, all I know, Nephew, is that possession is nine tenths of the law, and we are in possession of a contraption—maybe a machine left here by aliens from a faraway galaxy. I'll contact Bert over at the historical society. This may be some ancient artifact used by farmers back in the day for whatever purpose. Who knows. But then I can contact the owner of the orchard right next to us—I believe the McChesneys own it. Maybe he can fill us in on the mystery. But for sure this shed is on our property. Old Bill McChesney, a codger if there ever was one, will berate me, probably want the contents of the shed minus the rat smell. Oh, I'll just blow some magic cherry blend tobacco smoke in his face, charm his pants off, take him to the cleaners, and bid him *adieu*. I own this property now. Dig in those size twelve shoes—you and me we'll be in for a dog fight."

Nephew noticed a protuberance underneath the burlap bags. Reaching down he uncovered a hand, then a forearm, then a shoulder, finally a skull—but a skull with flesh still attached to the bone.

"Uncle, help me. What is this? The smell comes from here. What's this?"

The leaves and the burlap bags removed, a fleshed-out body lie there, face up, expression alarmed. Dead. Uncle alarmed, "Oh, crap. This body looks like it's been here a while. The body has decomposed. Some flesh left. I'll contact the Elk Rapids hospital. Now, I own this shed, its contents, and a body. I've hit the trifecta."

Nephew only flinched. "I'm just a teenager—what do I know, Uncle. Let me just have fun. I don't know what to say."

"I'll do my due diligence and contact Bert at the historical society. What do the McChesneys know. Should I keep Aunty in the dark? No, I can't. She reads me like a fine tooth comb. I'll take care of the details, Nephew. No need for you to get your panties in a bunch. The coroner's office first. Bert at the historical society second. Then Mr. McChesney. What with that landowner. Hush, hush, Nephew."

Later that day the body was removed to the Traverse City Coroner's Office. What was the cause of death? Who was this victim in the shed?

With Bob in tow, Uncle entered the hospital in Traverse, found where the sergeant who handled the case was located, and entered the room.

"Sit down, sir," said a curt voice. "And who might your buddy here be?"

"My nephew. He spotted the body you know marking off a plot of land for our new home." Uncle shifted nervously in his chair.

"Well, we were curt with you I know. We basically taped off the area, asked you a question or two, and sent you home. I asked you here to the hospital as we have identified the body. One Morris Tanner, an itinerant farmer, sometime inventor. He was not married, had no close relatives—none we could locate anyway. He used to work on the McChesney place doing odd jobs. That shed was where he worked to store his tools; that work bench provided him with space to lay out those tools, invent whatever. Our report from the coroner's office indicated he was struck on the skull with a blunt object—blunt force trauma was the cause of death. That weapon was not found in the shed. We're done with our time there. If that's your property you can do whatever with it now. We'll keep in touch. We have no suspects yet. Oh, Morris, the coroner's office states, had been dead for about a month more or less. A gruesome sight for you two to witness to be sure. And don't worry you're not persons of interest. That'll set your mind at ease, I'm sure. That contraption in there is a mighty strange looking device, er machine, or something old Morris was working on. Take care, you two. We'll be in touch if we find out any more information."

Uncle thanked the sergeant and left with Bob close behind. "Well, I'm certainly interested in that machine. I'll get Bert out to the shed. He'll be able to give a hint as to what that device is all about and maybe identify some of the tools on and in the drawers of that old wooden workbench."

Nephew spoke up: "This is a mystery, isn't it? Like a puzzle, having to put the pieces together. We don't know why he was killed. Maybe he had an argument about that strange machine. But with whom and why?"

"Say yer getting to be a regular detective yourself. Yes, there's someone out there who wanted Morris to be a goner, a mystery to be sure. Until that person is found, we all must be on our watch. You and I will be together fishing on the Big Lake in a few days. There's some big ones being caught out there—sundown, gray sky is the best time now to hook 'em on silver spoons. I got that tip from Doc Crowe. Fish between Deep Water and French Point, he said—one hundred thirty to one hundred fifty feet of water. You up to the task, young man?"

Bob grinned at Uncle: "This is what I came here for. Let's catch the biggest fish ever in the Big Lake."

"Why don't you spend the day tomorrow at the bridge with Pip and his work crew? Get the Lyman Islander cleaned up. Watch that diver at 4 PM. You can walk home—only three blocks from the bridge—and stop and say hi to Mr. Way. It isn't time for a haircut yet. You got a little mop on top of your head but not a full-blown bushel of hay yet. I wonder what Aunty is having for dinner. I think it's some form of stew. I taste an ice cream sundae on the porch this evening. We can see the baseball lights across the lake in Alden along the water. I hear Heater Hannigan's got a ninety-five mile an hour fastball. We'll believe it when we see it, right Nephew, er, Bob?" Bob felt secure again, but he knew now this would be the last season in The Big House.

He wondered what the new residence would be like. He heard his aunt once say to his uncle, "Give me a house and I'll make it into a home." He was sure this would be the way this new place would be like.

That shed, however, cast a shadow over that new property. He wanted to help solve the mystery—the puzzle. His mind was working overtime thinking, but tomorrow would be with Pip and his crew and Janina the diver. And he had to get the boat ready "shipshape" his uncle said for the big fishing expedition in a few days.

His summer days were now beginning to be filled with expectations and enjoyment. For the time being he could relax here at the Big Lake with Uncle and Aunty.

Chapter 4.

Bob Meets Janina's Younger Sister

At breakfast the next morning Uncle asked Nephew if he would first like to take a run over to the shed. Burt would be there and perhaps could explain what the contraption was all about. Then he could clean up the boat, help Pip turn the key on the bridge to open it when necessary, see the diver perform her act at 4 PM, then call it a day and get ready for the fishing trip tomorrow.

Bert was already at the shed, peeking in the dusty window when the two arrived. "Mornin' Bert; a bit chilly for this time of year," said Uncle, stoking up his pipe, bundled up in his goose-down jacket.

"Meet my nephew Bob. Bob—Bert; Bert—Bob." They shook hands.

"Thanks for comin'. Let's get inside, see what our tinkerer was tinkering about. Well, well we have a regular grab bag of toys. Here's a slide rule. There's some drafting pencils. Over here," he said, pointing toward the end of the bench, "we've got three compasses, various sizes, and some rulers metric and inches. It seems our tinkerer was doing more than tinkering. Ah-ha and by the bench—what is this, the contraption you were talking about." Bert picked up the entire load, then put it down in a hurry.

"No, this is not historical, my dear friends. This is a prototype. I suspect this is the start of some device to shake fruit, namely cherries, off the trees. This motor I'll bet vibrates." He flicked a switch. Nothing happened. "Well, if this motor could talk with the big rubber band attached, which would encircle the tree, it would say 'I'm a shakin', a rattlin,' and a rollin'—down come the cherries.' Sir, you have the do-ins to the future of the cherry business."

Uncle, taking the pipe out of his mouth, looking aghast spoke: "But then why didn't the killer take this rattletrap device, the drawings, and all the other paraphernalia—or was it just a random hit job?"

"I don't know," said Bert. "But I won't put it in our museum. Now all this stuff is yours."

"Maybe old Morris was going for a patent, had problems with a competitor, then boom—an argument. Morris was the victim; the perpetrator just got scared, took off in a flash, and disappeared into the night air.

"And there weren't any fingerprints of the killer and nothing was disturbed. Very odd, indeed," Uncle lamented.

"Well, it's all yours now. I'd say you'd better find a safe place for this machine and papers. I suspect word gets out—and maybe already has—what this machine might be, they'll be a flock of people wantin' to put their hands on it."

With those words, Bert left. Uncle and Nephew were left to decide what to do.

"Give me a hand with all these instruments, drawings, and papers, Bob. I'll drag the contraption to the truck. Both of us can lift it up."

"So now we really have a mystery, Uncle. But maybe what

you and Bert were talking about provides a motive," Bob spoke up.

"Good reasoning, Nephew. I know Aunty will question me as to what all this is about. She'll be on my case with questions. I know I can secure all this stuff in our shed out back. I can lock it up pretty tight.

"But we gotta keep quiet, understand? We'll keep our eyes and ears open as to who might be starting to create these types of devices.

"The police are on the case. Let's hope they come up with some possible leads. Don't say a word to anyone even if they happen to question you. It seems every type of crime is reported in that Elk Rapids rag sheet. Have we got a deal?"

Bob looked up at his uncle and smiled, the smoke now billowing skyward from his pipe. "Yes, we gotta deal."

"Good, now let's get you back home, unload our prize, lock it up, and you can have the rest of the day to yourself.

"Yes sir, sky is getting grayer and grayer; wind coming from the south; spoons are in; one hundred thirty feet of water, big lake trout waiting to be caught . . . a record catch.

"A trollin' we will go, a trollin' we will go, hi ho the dairy oh, a trollin' we will go."

The marina was bustling with activity. It was early in the season, and boaters were getting their boats out of storage, charging them up, and taking them on test runs.

Uncle's boat was already cranked down from a storage loft in one of the bays. He had, at the beginning of the season, taken it out into the Big Lake and once down the river on a fishing trip with other resort owners to Round Lake.

Bob knew where the large bucket was located. *Fill it with lukewarm water; find the white vinegar; mix it in with the water, find the scrub brush, and get to work.* He had been here with Uncle last year and as he put it, "You'll learn the ropes cleaning my pride and joy."

He remembered what Uncle said about the dimensions of this craft, the materials used to build it, and why he chose this kind of boat. The model was a Lyman Islander—all mahogany, six cylinders, eighteen feet long. It was, as Uncle said, a scenic cruiser capable of hosting six passengers, a cruising speed of twenty knots.

It was fitted for fishing, two outrigger lines tested at over a hundred pounds. When trolling, the craft could run silent at four knots per hour.

Bob scrubbed the interior of the boat. He made sure not to splash liquid around the dials up front. He knew tomorrow he would be guiding the boat out in deep waters like on some super highway.

If Uncle hooked a fish maybe he thought he would be allowed to "play" with it for a while. In two previous outings on the lake no fish was hooked—once a log was pulled up. Uncle knew it was just brush as he said, "That varmit had no life in it—must be some old lifeless sea creature." He knew all the time it was just a piece of a junk pile brought up as some great underwater treasure.

This sort of jostling humor wouldn't fool Bob this time. He wanted badly to hook a big one, a real prize winner, bring it to the marina in the middle of the night, and have his picture taken. The headlines would read *prize-winning fish—biggest ever since first recorded caught in the Big Lake.*

"Hey, kid, ya got your uncle's craft all shined up. You going to a rodeo?"

Bob was shaken out of his dream. "Oh hi, Pip. Yeah, I'm going out with Uncle tomorrow up past the point." He stopped mid-sentence, thinking not to divulge the route Uncle told him about.

"Well, we need help on the bridge in an hour or so. The Judge Jr. scenic cruiser is chugging this way. We could use an extra hand on deck," said Pip smiling, knowing Bob to be eager to help.

"Okay, as soon as I finish cleaning this chrome, I'll be outta here."

"Hey, and I want you to meet a new friend who's hanging around the docks this summer. Come out when yer done." Pip scampered out of the boathouse.

The sky was darkening. The wind, as Uncle had said, was shifting, coming across the lake from east to west, an unusual direction. Uncle claimed this direction would stir up the calcium carbonate and other sediment. This may be an "old wive's tale" he said, but the bigger fish seem to bite when these conditions take place.

Today, there was Pip, Big Stan, Freaky Fred, and Baby Huey on the key. These men all worked at the marina in one capacity or another.

The Judge, fast approaching, sounded its horn. With the key in place, the bridge creaked and groaned, moving ever so slowly. At forty-five degrees, it stopped. The judge barely slipped through. Passengers on board waved to the workers and those people on the boardwalk tending to their business. After turning the bridge back, it took three workers to drag the key to its place just off the bridge. It would be used again when The Judge returned from its trip up the river and around Lake Skegamog and back.

Bob was walking on the boardwalk when Janina approached. "Hey, Tiger, good to see you out from your hiding place over by the pilings in that enchanted marsh of yours."

"Hi," he said, startled, and turned to see her already in her suit waiting for her daily four o'clock jump from the highest cable on the bridge.

"Ya, I just came here today to polish Uncle's boat. We're taking it out tomorrow to troll. The fishing is supposed to be good, the conditions being what they are."

"You'd better wear your rain gear tomorrow. It's going to be a stormy day. I won't dive in that kind of weather."

As she came closer to Bob, he noticed her already tanned body, her freckles even turning to darker spots.

"Say, Bob, I want you to meet my younger sister. These past few seasons she's had to stay home. That darn ballet company occupied most of her summers. But this season she's decided to take time off from the rigors and stress—all that competition has taken its toll.

"Here she is. Over here, Heather. I want you to meet Bob—his uncle and aunt own the resort right over there," she said, point-

ing in a northward direction to a beach on the other side of the bridge.

"We Junkers are in competition, but friends are friends. Right, Bob?" Janina smiled, her face lighting up. Bob's attention focused on the dimples on Janina's face.

"Oh right. Hello, Heather. Glad to make your acquaintance," Bob put out a formal welcome.

Heather approached him, sizing him up. "Cut the formality. A friend of sis' is a friend of mine. You here to watch sis dive?"

"That and getting Uncle's Lyman Islander ready for a fishing trip tomorrow." As Heather came closer, he noticed freckles similar to Janina's but not quite so dark. Nor was her skin tanned yet. He learned this was her first week at her own uncle and aunt's resort—Junkers Resort.

"I had to cool it for a summer season. The ballet business got to me. I don't want to burn out. I'm up for the lead in The Nutcracker this Christmas season. I want to be at my peak then. Maybe we'll all get together at our family's summer barbecue for the community week after next over the 4th of July at the Community Park. Are you going to be here then?"

"I should be. That'll be fun. Thanks for the offer." Bob stuttered a bit and backed away slightly from Heather. She seemed to be totally at ease with herself and unaffected by his hesitant movement. Thinking Heather to be done talking, he started walking down the boardwalk toward the bridge only to hear, "Remember, I'm a ballet dancer. I can outswim Janina any day of the week. Strong leg kick don't ya know. She outpaces me with her diving. I out-pace her with my swimming stroke. See you soon."

Heather left heading toward the marina's gift shop, not stopping to watch her older sister's dive.

Janina had left a minute earlier to begin the ascent up to the highest cable span, a daily ritual—4 PM approached.

Bob's mind raced. Two ladies today talking to him—adult to adult. For Heather, unabashed and completely natural; Janina is sociable, friendly, but just an acquaintance. How old was Heather? He surmised thirteen, fourteen. Bob, a year or two older. Janina, much older—late twenties.

Now was it possible age was a factor in different kinds of relationships? He said the term to himself—"the opposite sex."

Bob moved onto the bridge taking small steps across it as he moved. Janina was now at the top waiting for the all-clear signal from Pip below. She started her dive, body spiraling into the emerald-colored current below—a perfect execution. Bob continued walking across the bridge not acknowledging Janina as she pulled herself up out of the water at the boardwalk.

He was on his way, one last stop at Dan's market before ending this day—this day of freedom.

"Well hello, young man, c'mon in. Make yourself at home." The market was busy, and Dan was cutting meat, packaging the individual parts, passing these packages to an assistant for checkout, whom Bob didn't recognize.

"I've got your crate warmed up to make your bottom happy; sit a spell. I've got these customers to satisfy first." Dan, always at ease, smiled at his customers. His motto 'Dan's the Man to give great service and his meat is a treat to eat.' This saying was posted on the outside window of the store.

"Now I've got time for ya," said Dan, out of breath. He sat on a chair next to Bob. "Yer gettin' bigger every day. I hear you helped your uncle plot off some land up Torch Lake Drive. I know your uncle and aunt are planning to sell the resort. A shame I say. They really helped my business, not just sellin' meat and cheese, but adding a sundries section to the store, your aunt's suggestion. Everyone needs toothpaste, soap, lotions and potions—even cough drops and bowel movement items. Don't mean to get too personal there. Hey how about that Hannigan over in Alden. Comes from a good family. The scouts are after him. I know your uncle takes you over there from time to time."

Bob finally spoke up, sensing Dan had run out of breath momentarily: "Maybe someday I'll own a business like yours, serving customers' needs. I can't think of what it might be yet. I see many happy people come to your market and leave happy also. I have a question, maybe a favor to ask. Do you or your other butcher fillet big fish? Tomorrow, Uncle and I are going trolling out in the Big Lake. The conditions are right for the big ones, the lake trout, to bite. Uncle says he's never seen better conditions." Now he stopped and waited for a response.

Dan let out a chuckle: "So your uncle says this is the best time he's seen, huh. Well, he's seen 'em pull in some big ones over the past week and weigh 'em down at the marina. Some of those lake trout are approaching record weights and sizes. Something about the calcium carbonate being stirred up making the big ones restless. But, yes, I do have a butcher on staff who'll fillet those big ones for ya, make 'em into steaks. Nothing better than fresh fillet of trout, especially lake trout. Bread 'em if you like. Pan-fried or on the grill. Now you're makin' me salivate, young man.

Well, I got some work to do in the freezer; got it all electrified. Did the rewiring myself. A great job if I do say so myself—and I do. I'll see you day after tomorrow with that big one that didn't get away."

Nephew got up from his sitting box and smiled at Dan. Dan came over and gave Bob a big hug. "Next time I'll take you into the freezer and give you a tour of the inner workings—show you all the fresh game hanging on special hooks that the hunters have brought in. Betcha didn't think muskrat was good eatin'. They'll be a wild game dinner over at Persons Harbor in a couple of weeks. If you're still in these parts, ask Uncle and Aunty to take you there for some real mouth-watering treats. Hook 'em hard tomorrow. You'll be wearin' your rain slickers. Uncle won't be able to keep his pipe lit." At this last comment, he let out a belly laugh.

Bob left to get back to The Big House. He knew he wouldn't sleep well as excited as he was already. The skies were getting more ominous. Dan was right. He and Uncle would be bundled up trying to stay as comfortable as possible.

The Lyman Islander was an open vessel. A good boat for trolling but provided no protection from inclement weather.

Before everyone went to bed, Uncle sat Bob down and caught him up on the killing of Morris Tanner.

"There's really no word from our county's sheriff as to who might be a suspect. Seems there's rumors going 'round that one of those migrants may have done Morris in, but those are just rumors. I took that contraption, the slide rules, the diagrams, and other paperwork over to the county sheriff. It's evidence anyway, and I don't want it in my shed. Never know who'll come snoopin' 'round wanting to steal that machine.

"That old farmer McChesney is might quiet about all this commotion. He knows more than he's letting on. But he did acknowledge the shed is on my property. Do with it as you will. It's no longer a crime scene. Later this week I'm knockin' it down. Aunty got her bun in a bunch about all this attention. Ladies at Persons Harbor are spreading gossip like wildfire. Seems every one of those ladies knows some ne'er-do-well who's capable of bludgeoning someone into the next world.

"I know you want to go to that Daniel's shindig next week; Aunty was tellin' me. Gotta be careful, Bob. We'll talk about it later in the week. Meanwhile, get some sleep. Tomorrow, rain or shine, we'll be on the lake trollin' for the big one." Uncle, sleepy-eyed, headed to bed. This time Bob stepped forward and hugged his uncle.

"Thanks for letting me in on all that's going on. I cleaned up the boat spic and span, even cleaned the metal trim. I also hooked up the Northwind resort flag. We'll catch a record tomorrow." Bob's voice trailed off as he went down the hallway to his bedroom.

Uncle with the last word, "That is if we don't catch a death of cold in all that rain."

Chapter 5.

Fishing on the Big Lake—

Catch of the Day (maybe the season)

The afternoon rain was getting more intense, pelting the tin roof of the boathouse. There was now some question as to whether the two would venture out onto the lake whose waters were getting choppier and choppier.

Uncle spoke: "As long as we're sittin' and waitin' for some relief out there, I want you to see my tacklebox, inside a plethora—how's that word—of ways to hook 'em before ya cook 'em."

Bob peered into the large four-tiered box to discover spoons, plugs, jerkbaits, shiners, spools of line, nylon string-hooks, treble and otherwise, sinkers, bobbers, flies, and various cleaning agents to keep the poles clean.

"Like what you see? We'll use a pair of seven-foot rods—one on each insert—and a little more than a hundred feet of line, forty to fifty pound test line.

"We'll fish more into shore, maybe ninety to a hundred feet of water. Got all that? We'll use some spoon spinners, different colors, blue, silver, orange, pink. You're my driver. We'll troll at almost three miles per hour. If we hook one you're gonna be on the line for a while. We've got a gaff hook and a net if we need one."

Uncle glanced out at the glowering sky. He noticed a break in the clouds. "Let's get our act together. Full steam ahead."

The Islander started and backed out of the boathouse around a few other buildings through a narrow channel onto the river toward the bridge—then under the bridge out into open waters. The sky was a stark gray, and winds blew east to west, past the two-mile sandbar now out into some of the deepest part of the lake on a direct route to Deepwater Point.

Uncle steered the craft past Doc Crowes place then spoke to Nephew: "No time like the present to learn to steer this tub. Get on the wheel. Keep the speed between two and three miles per hour. Head in a straight line toward the point.

"I'm droppin' the line in, lettin' it out. If we get a hit, I'll reel it in for a while, then I'll let you have a hand at it. I'll guide you as we go. Now we'll be patient and wait."

Both remained quiet as the craft made its way toward the point. After a half hour of trolling, it reached the point. "Keep steering . . . doin' okay. Head in a straight line toward French Point," said Uncle, now with a pipe in his mouth, needing to relight. He remained calm, turning once to brush Bob's hair, stroking it with the palm of his hand.

"Gettin' dark, young man. A few more minutes and we'll turn around and head back. Maybe I'll reel in and try another color jerkbait."

Nephew now sensed boredom setting in and his attention was less focused. The rain had stopped, but he was wet, water coming through his rain gear. He altered his position between standing and sitting on a soaked cushion.

"Get out that beef jerky and oatmeal raisin cookie from the snack bag Aunty gave us. You need a pick-me-up," said Uncle, sensing Bob beginning to get drowsy and his attention waning.

"How much longer? It's almost dark. I'm getting cold. My stomach is upset." He finished the jerky and cookie and sat down again on the wet cushion.

"Okay, make a u-turn. We're headin' back. Just go out about ten more feet before you turn. Aunty is probably wonderin' when we're comin' home. No dinner tonight."

The east to west wind died down, and the lake was ominously quiet. There were no other trollers around. Nephew sensed they were out in the middle of nowhere, alone, just the two of them—the protector and the young boy, as Uncle put it, "learning the ropes."

The strike came fast and unexpectedly. The rod bent in half. Uncle's pipe flew out of his mouth as he grabbed the reel and pulled on the rod. There was now slack. He took in some line. The initial hit was over. The fight began—fish versus fisherman.

"Keep it steady, Nephew. No more than three miles per hour. She's layin' low here a while till she figures out what she's done. Don't know yet if the old gal's been really hooked well or not. I'll reel in some more slack." Uncle remained standing, waiting for more fight.

Bob's stomach churned. Goosebumps appeared on his neck and arms. He thought he was getting sick yet another feeling—exhilaration—flooded his body and his head spun like an out-of-control top.

Uncle continued the progression of reeling in the slack, letting the fish tire out as it thrashed about now less than fifty feet from the surface. "Here, take the rod. You watched how I handled her. You know what to do," he said as Bob nodded and took charge.

He waited until he thought the fish was tired, or maybe, he thought, just waiting to snap the lure out of his mouth—the big one that got away.

Doubts crept into his already squeamish self. *Be careful, but not too careful. Maybe turn this job back over to Uncle.*

"Good job, Nephew. She's a comin' up the surface. We'll have a look at her in a minute or so."

Then, like a rocket, the fish emerged, its long sleek body still struggling to free itself from the bait, the spoon deeply imbedded in its throat.

"Now, Nephew, you can handle the net. Give me the rod. I'll get it close to the boat. You scoop it into the net. Don't worry, we got this. Just stop the engine, young man. Okay, it's layin' flat on the surface. Careful, get it all in the net. Good, good. Together now. Let's get it in the boat. Both pulled up the fish, flapping and still fighting for its life.

"She's a mammoth lake trout alright. I'll get her in the cooler. It hardly fits, son."

Both fishermen were out of breath; the old, wizened veteran and his newly-appointed apprentice.

"How'd I do? I followed your orders, Uncle. We did it. It's a big one, isn't it? It's a real keeper, right Uncle?" Nephew was now all smiles.

"You did more than follow orders. You had a fine feel for gettin' this job done—landing her. You—we—won this battle. But let me tell you, there are times out here fishing and all when we'll let the fish go back to fight another day. This one we'll weigh in at the marina, let Dan's butcher fillet it, have a few meals with some of Aunty's fixins'; or maybe better yet we'll take the fillet to Persons Harbor, that craft fair comin' up, and let the whole community enjoy our catch."

Uncle found his pipe on the floor of the boat and placed it in his mouth, grinning as he looked out at the vast expanse of the lake—the night sky appeared. With the lights of the boat now turned on, both expert and novice headed back to the marina to weigh the catch of the day—maybe the season.

The old codgers, as Uncle called them, pulled up the fish and took it to the scale.

"We'll be back in a flash." Uncle smiled at these old-timers who, at this time of night, made it a habit to gawk or smirk at the catches coming in.

Bob and Uncle muscled their way to the scale. "Yes sir, a real catch I'd say, fifty-six pounds fourteen ounces. No record but a mighty pretty lady," said Shorty Lantz, self-proclaimed bearer of the yardstick, speaking to the throng now gathering at the scale.

"Uncle and I fought this monster as we were about ready to call it quits. Right, Uncle?"

Before Uncle could speak, Bob continued, "We used a special spoon. We hooked him good. I steered the boat then Uncle let me pull him in."

"Say, why did you call our fish *lady*?" Bob asked, looking at Shorty.

"Because, young man, she has a short, rounded nose; same with the upper jaw. She's had many seasons of spawning I can tell. This un's about forty years old. Out in the deep part of the lake, many years. She's got many of her offspring out there. Quite the mama fish," he said, his voice trailing off. Others nodded in agreement.

Suddenly, Bob's stomach churned. So, Uncle and I killed a mother. This fish was just minding its business when we came along and tricked it into biting a piece of silver with hooks on it.

Uncle came over and gave Bob a pat on the head. "Son, that's nature out there. I told you we let a lot of fish go back to their home. This one's had a good life. It'll provide many meals at the craft fair comin' up. We'll keep it on ice for a while—they'll take it to Dan's market. It'll be filleted. Now let's get home. Get some rest. You got some party to go to over at the shantytown with your friend Daniel.

We'll talk about it all in the morning. Got some more news about the death of old Morris. Tell ya in the morning."

Chapter 6.

A Celebration—Isabella's Quinceañera

That following morning at breakfast Uncle filled Bob in concerning the death of Morris Tanner.

"I see Aunty has you clean and shaven for that migrant girl's coming out party—isn't it her fifteenth birthday? I wonder what she's comin' out to?" Uncle smiled, knowing he was testing Nephew's patience.

"I was invited by Daniel," Bob spoke up. "He said I'll learn a lot about the Mexican culture. The whole village will be going. It's a big event for their community," said Nephew, showing some agitation.

"Okay, okay, I was only pulling your leg. Anyways, news about that Tanner body . . . seems maybe he had a feud with Bill McChesney's brother Cecil. That contraption was only one of the arguments. It seems Morris had other inventions that Cecil wanted part of. Something about some kind of machine that lifted golf balls out of ponds on golf courses. Morris was also working on some sort of organic fertilizer for the orchards, which wouldn't pollute the rivers and lakes. There's a lot of run-off in these parts of fertilizer, which gets into the rivers and streams; it's beginning to pollute the Big Lake.

"Anyway, Cecil was seen. Got a witness at that shack maybe the day Morris was killed. Just sayin' the police are chasin' down clues. Maybe he's the culprit, maybe not."

"Thanks for the update. Daniel said I could come over a little early. I'm ready," said Bob, starting for the truck.

Uncle brushed his head with the palm of his hand. "You're growin' some summer curls, and the back of your head looks like a big old brush pile. Time to go to Bob the barber. He set up shop, you know, right next to Dan's place. Don't ya know—two butchers in one neighborhood. Don't that beat all." Uncle now doubled over clutching his stomach.

"Well, let's get you to the party. Have some fun. Ya catch some look see at the ladies today. Bye, Aunty. Ya he'll be on his best behavior. He's got some lady friends to impress," said Uncle again doubling over with laughter.

The Mexican shantytown was just a few miles up a steep road, left turn at the Kewadin sign, down a dirt road where the town consisted of several tarred shacks, six trailers—home to the larger families—several trucks—most being worked on—and one large screened-in building built by the men here—made of stone, bricks, lumber hauled in from area construction sites, and plumbing made up of pipes, faucets, basins, etc., and homemade urinals and toilets suitable for large crowds for the many special occasions occurring here in this village.

Today the decorations were bountiful—all colors of streamers and flags flying on poles and clotheslines along a main street could be seen as a tribute to one Isabella Ortez, age fifteen, her Quinceañera—or coming-out party—about to begin on this sunny, hospitable early June afternoon.

As Bob jumped from the truck, he was met by Daniel who

grasped his arm and greeted him warmly. "Welcome, señor Bob. Come, come let me introduce you to my family on this glorious day for my sister."

Uncle's truck turned around. He waved and smiled at Bob. He would return by 9:00 PM.

Both walked along the dusty street. They reached the community center building.

"Most of the activities will be inside, but you see over there—a park-like clearing—a large piñata hanging from an old oak tree; that is where the young ones will be this afternoon knocking it apart. There are many valuable prizes inside.

"Ah, here are my other sisters. My brother Pedro is twelve; he's helping Mama with party favors. Juanita is ten; Carmen is eight; and Angel is six. Sisters, meet my friend Bob. He will be with us today to celebrate Isabella's coming out."

The three girls giggled as they said their hellos.

"Pleased to meet you, ladies." Bob thought the more formal approach to be best.

Juanita spoke for the group: "We are pleased to make your acquaintance. Please do enjoy our party and the food. Please, maybe we teach you a dance step or two. There will be a dance of the old men today at the general dance—but I see you are not old. Just watch them to learn the steps." Juanita knew she misspoke and giggled—the other two girls chimed in with a giggle.

"Oh, Bob can learn the Mexican hat dance. Steps taught by our cousin Renaldo," Daniel broke in. "See you at the party," the three girls spoke in unison as they headed for the community building.

Daniel continued: "Let me fill you in on this tradition of our people. At the age of fifteen our sisters have what is called a coming-out party. We are following the Aztec tradition of many hundreds of years ago when the young maidens would have such a party. This would signify their time to start looking for a husband and a time for these maidens to be considered adults. Back then, our people did not live that long, so the age of fifteen was chosen. Today fifteen is so young, but our sisters are leaving their childhood and entering young adulthood. They will have to wait some years after this party to find a marriage partner. Anyway, let's go inside where we can sit, and I can explain what is going to happen."

Daniel and Bob found a space in the corner. Bob observed the long tables being decorated with bright flowers and runners of gold, green, and yellow. He suddenly thought this whole community showed up on this special day for Isabella.

"First Isabella will walk in here through an archway decorated with her favorite flowers. Papa will give a toast. Papa will have the first dance. Isabella has chosen the song, "Earth Angel." Then our family will dance. Then you, Bob, can dance. I'm sure someone will choose you. Oh, there will be the Mexican hat dance, and our elders will dance the "Dance of the Old Men." Then we will sit down at these long tables to eat chimichangas, enchiladas, fajitas, and tacos from my mama's kitchen. So, enjoy the day, Bob, my friend. After we eat, the younger boys and girls will go to the park and knock the stuffings out of the piñata. Oh, tonight at dark, hope you can stay; we have special fireworks exploding over our village. When your uncle comes to pick you up, please tell him to stay for the fireworks. Quite a celebration, eh amigo."

"I just thought of something, Daniel," Bob broke in. "Isabella and I are the same age. Is there a similar celebration for young boys going into manhood?"

"No, but we are given more work to do. It won't be long till I will be expected to work harder—pick more fruit, "carry my weight" Papa says. But I have plans, Bob. I know an education will be good for me. I can maybe go on to a college—learn to work with my mind. I have studied already about machinery and new types of inventions, which will help our people and make life easier for all of us. I go to the Elk Rapids library and find books about motors, gears, big machines and small. I can fix the engines in our trucks here in our village, make them run better and save our people money. That is why I listen carefully to the teachers from Persons Harbor. They teach me to read but also to understand what I am reading and to apply it to solve problems—especially mechanical problems."

"Good for you, Daniel. I go to our public school downstate and also enjoy reading about new inventions to help make our lives easier and better. When I am eighteen my father says I can have a car, but I must save most of the money by working. I have a paper route. I mow lawns for money. I have an allowance, and I help my father with his business and he pays me a little amount."

This conversation ended abruptly as Isabella, dressed in a lacy white gown, clutching a small purse, began her stroll under the flowery trellis. She walked the full length of the community building ending her walk at a stage where various electronic gear was plugged in.

Everyone sitting at the long tables stopped to focus their attention on Isabella as she smiled at her family, friends, and acquaintances. Her sisters and brothers along with Daniel were now at the head table. Bob was at a table nearby, a spectator enveloped by the pageantry and tradition.

Her father was first to speak. "Thank you all for coming to Isabella's Quinceañera, her coming of age party. We are all family here. Please enjoy this tradition and enjoy the festivities." He put the microphone down and began to dance to the song she chose, "Earth Angel."

The second dance, "Unforgettable," was for the family. The disc jockey started to pick other songs as other people gathered on the floor to begin dancing. Bob sat for a few dances. On the fourth dance, Juanita came over to coax him out on the floor. They danced to a slow tune, and he returned to his seat. Suddenly, four elders of the village stood and started to gyrate to a fast-paced melody.

Daniel, who was now again sitting next to Bob, proclaimed this to be the "Dance of the Old Men." The entire crowd laughed in unison as the men flailed their arms and legs in a scattered fashion—slowing down steadily, finally crouching low, then dropping to their knees at the end of their routine.

The applause was deafening. Hector spoke again. "Please, eat our food—partake in the tres leches cake. The children will knock at the piñata after we eat.

"There will be one more tradition after dinner—the Mexican hat dance. We have most of our performers, all but two friends of our family to choose. Now I point to you over there sitting by Daniel. Your name is Bob, am I right?"

Bob blushed, "Yes, I am Bob." He felt the stares of everyone. He wanted to hide under the table and disappear. He just wanted to be an observer. Now he would be a participant, and all eyes would be on his performance—this Mexican hat dance.

"And for our second guest dancer," Hector again spoke as he looked toward the back wall, "I choose you. What is your name, young lady?" The young girl in the corner stood up, smiled, and spoke out for all the crowd to hear. "My name is Heather Junker."

Bob peered over at the far end of the hall. *Could this be true? That is Janina's younger sister. And I am going to be out in front of everyone dancing—or whatever I will be doing—following directions to that song.* His stomach churned as he tried to eat his food. *Why was this dance done after the meal?* Another tradition he supposed.

A large Mexican hat was placed on the floor. Four close friends of Isabella surrounded the hat. Isabella sat on a throne-like chair to watch the participants. One of the friends turned to Bob and Heather to instruct them on how to move.

"Right arm up, left arm down. Hands on hips, right foot hop to left. Clap, clap, clap," instructed one of the friends, looking at Bob and Heather. Both nodded.

The music started, and the group in unison moved around the hat. The dance lasted a few minutes as onlookers clapped along with the dancers. The music stopped, and Heather approached Bob. Smiling, she said, "You've got some moves there."

Bob, nervously, smiled back. "I just follow directions well."

"There go the kids, outside to knock down the piñata." Heather headed outside, and Bob followed as she carried on the conversation.

"My uncle brought me over. Daniel is my friend. He invited me. I like this tradition. I am as old as Isabella. Daniel told me what Quinceañera means. Every fifteen-year-old girl has this coming-out party," said Bob, keeping up the conversation.

Several children began taking swipes at the piñata, one or two hitting it directly, causing several pounds of candy to fall to the ground. A scramble followed, and giggling, laughing children fell to the ground, grabbing the candy and stuffing pieces into their pants pockets. Some of the girls gripped small bags and were filling them up with sweets.

"Aren't children a blessing? So eager for fun?" said Heather, noticing the children falling all over themselves with joy and laughter.

"Oh, yes," said Bob, blushing, "and children are so young." He realized his comment was somewhat foolish and blushed even more—more crimson red.

Heather laughed, her deep dimples exploding. Turning to Bob, she said, "You certainly have a way with the English language. Anyway, I liked the way you got into the dance. That was a first for both of us. It's been a fun day. I'm glad we could share part of it together."

Bob, still flushed, said, "Thank you, Heather. It'll be dark soon. The fireworks are about to start. I wonder where my uncle is? And I have to thank Daniel for inviting me. I see Isabella is with the children. Boy, there certainly were a lot of goodies in that piñata." He managed to gush out several thoughts in a single breath.

"Stay with me until your uncle comes to pick you up," she said, coming closer to Bob. He now noticed her freckles and her hair cascading down her shoulders. Her eyes sparkled and her smile sent his heart racing.

It was now dark, and an announcement was made that the fireworks were to begin. A crowd gathered at the park. The night air was cool but comfortable. The stars twinkled, and the fireworks began.

Heather covered her ears during the loud explosive missiles. She reached over and clutched her hand in Bob's. He in turn held her hand firmly, but not too tight.

What were the rules with hand holding? The bright expressive fireworks lit up the sky. The crowd reacted with *oohs* and *aahs*. At the end the crowd is dispersed. Heather and Bob walked together back to the community center.

"Maybe I'll see you at the craft fair at Persons Harbor next weekend," Heather smiled at Bob—both were toe to toe.

"Oh, I go where my uncle and aunt go. I think I'll still be here. Okay, maybe I'll see you there." He realized that was not a very independent statement. But then he really couldn't go wherever he wanted whenever he wanted.

Just then, Uncle's truck pulled up, and he honked his horn. Bob found Daniel and thanked him. Heather was gone. "Congratulations on your celebration," he managed to almost shout at Isabella.

Daniel's parents were nowhere to be found so he hopped in the truck. His uncle smiled, eager to ask Bob how his day's activities went.

"So, you got to know the Ortez family and this tradition of 'coming out.'" Bob was grilled all the way home. In his room, he reflected on the day's activities—the food, the dancing, all the traditions, but most of all his meeting again with Heather. She seemed to take an interest in him and was not shy to express that interest. And she wanted to see him again. He thought he would still be with his uncle and aunt the next weekend. He was sure he would attend the Persons Harbor fair with his uncle and aunt.

He saw his aunt prepare jampot jelly preserve to take there, and she mentioned she would be bringing a mixed fruit and bread pudding.

He wished he were older and had "wheels" so he could be more independent.

The following day was dump day, and Uncle had many scraps from a construction site to clean up. Also, that small barn on the new property Uncle owned was to be knocked down and was to be removed.

As he dozed off, he thought of Heather's sparkling eyes, green in color he thought, and some scent from some sweet-smelling flower came his way as he stood next to her holding her hand during the display of fireworks.

He woke the next morning to the smell of bacon, pancakes grilling, and jampot jam on the table waiting to be slathered on homemade biscuits.

Chapter 7.

A Fire—Prominent Member of the Community Succumbs

After breakfast Uncle took Bob aside and asked him to sit and listen for a minute before they set out to the dumpsite.

"First, that shed is going to be taken away by a crew I hired. There are too many pieces of rotted wood and debris for us to haul down the side of that property you marked off. We'll just go to that site on the water and load all the junk on the truck and make one trip to the dump. Second, and here comes some bad news, your friend Daniel has been summoned for questioning about the death of Morris Tanner. It seems he was seen at the shed perhaps the night Morris was killed."

Bob spoke up, "Oh, come on. He's just a young boy—younger than me. He comes from a good family. He wouldn't hurt anyone—honest Uncle."

"Well, the police found a list of food items to be purchased at Dan's Market at that site with the name Hector, Daniel's father's name, at the bottom of the note. Apparently, he wandered up the road, out of curiosity, saw that shed and went inside. Also, one of the McChesney clan told police there was some kind of ruckus that night over in the shed. What Daniel was doing there is anybody's guess."

"But that's absurd. Just accusations. We found that body. The coroner said he had been dead up to a month."

"Someone's trying to . . . what's the word . . . *frame* him," came Uncle's reply.

"Yes, as you say Uncle, something is fishy. It doesn't make sense."

"Well, all I know is that early this morning Daniel and his father were questioned about the murder. You got up late this morning. A lot has happened. I got a call from my source at the sheriff's office. I suspect there was a lot of arguing and hatred going on between Morris and members of the McChesney clan. They're trying to cover their tracks . . . put the blame for the killin' on someone else. Daniel may have been at the wrong place at the wrong time. I still think it has something to do with those inventions—that cherry shaker and that golf ball machine—maybe some other inventions Morris was brewing up. They let Daniel go of course, but he remains a person of interest—but what a shame. Yes, they are a good family and all, but when some community members get wind that a migrant was breaking into a shed and a death occurred, they'll put two and two together and come up with five. But there are those who don't like the migrants, who look down on them—their itinerant nature and all—and will blame young Daniel for the death. Remember, too, the McChesney's have a lot of pull in these parts. They're a powerful bunch of rascals I say; best just try to avoid them if possible. I hope I don't have any trouble with our lot we just purchased. You marked it carefully, I'm sure. They'll start the foundation for our new home later in the summer. Hopefully, the framing will be up, and it'll be almost completed before the bad snow flies. Come on then. To the dump. Tell Aunty goodbye. You got her jam all over your mush." Both smiled at each other as they went out the back door to the truck for a working man's day to the county dump.

The evening sky turned a crimson color.

"Red sky at night, sailor's delight," Uncle spoke while sitting on the screened-in front porch.

"What do you give two tired working men at the end of a long day of dust and grime?" He turned toward Aunty—the pipe coming out of his mouth." He tapped it twice on the ash tray.

"A large chocolate sundae, whipped cream on the top. A big juicy cherry on top of the whipped cream," Aunty replied quickly.

The three of them sat watching the Big Lake calm down, the puttering sound of motors heading toward the marina.

"Still got a gentle easterly breeze out there; fishin' might still be good up the points. We got our catch didn't we Bob? Those fillets will be served at the craft fair in a few days. Aunty's bringin' her jam and other goodies. He peered over and saw Aunty doing some knitting. "Didn't know you were doing some needlework."

"I'm knitting some booties for a couple of babies, migrant ones, just born. And I'm makin' a hat for one of them," Aunty replied.

"Girlie, you never cease to amaze me. I gotta lady who can cook, clean, and do knitting, too. What a combination. I hit the mother load when we got hitched.

"I know our view of the lake at our new home will be just as wondrous as it is now. We're gonna be higher up on a hill. We've got beach access. And don't forget no more rentin' these cottages. That'll be a relief for both of us, especially your back."

It was now pitch dark except for a dimly-lit lamp by Uncle. Aunty put away her knitting. Bob, the slowest to finish his sundae, placed his dish on the table next to him.

A strange yellow glow burst into the sky not far from the marina. Uncle stood up, perplexed, and peered at the glow. "I'll be a monkey's uncle. It looks like something's burning over in that neighborhood just east of the marina. Now there's some smoke and flames."

Aunty got up as did Bob. She shouted out, "I think a building is on fire. I think I hear sirens. Something is not right."

"I've got to go over there and see what it's all about," said Uncle, opening the screen door and racing to his truck. "I always keep my keys in my pocket," he thought. *Hurry up.*

Bob followed close on his heels. Uncle shouted back at Aunty still on the porch. "Hold down the fort! We won't be gone long."

A large gathering surrounded the house, now engulfed in flames. Police had roped off an area keeping the spectators back. An EMT carried a body out, placing it in the van.

Uncle, startled, recognized this residence. He had visited this place many times; played cards with the owner; talked about the problems of starting up a small business and keeping it going. This residence was a pillar in the community. He used his business sense to help those in need, namely the migrant popula-

tion that inhabited the area during the picking season. He made friends easily with young and old alike.

Uncle and Bob got out of the truck to survey the scene. Uncle cried out, "This is Dan Way's home. Is that Dan being carried on that stretcher? What in Heaven's name is going on?"

Suddenly, the wind changed directions, and Uncle and Bob nearly choked out on the smoke. "Move over there, Bob," said Uncle, pointing to a grove of trees away from the smoke.

The onlookers were mumbling to themselves and those close around. One spoke up, "I'm their neighbor. I just started seeing the fire in the back of the house; our back doors are adjacent to each other. I'm about fifty yards away. He's got a big lot don't ya know. The whole back half of the house is gone. Must have been a propane explosion or an electrical fire. You know his wife and two children are on a shopping trip to Traverse. Just old Dan there minding the store."

"Okay, folks, break it up. Nothing to see. Back to your homes. We have to rope off this whole area, find out what happened. Oh hi, Unc'," said the fire chief, noticing Uncle in the crowd. "See you got your nephew with you. This is certainly a tragedy all right. Dan's an upright guy. No one ever said a bad word about him. Hope he's okay but doesn't look good. I'll let you know tomorrow how he's doing."

Everyone now was heading back to their cars and trucks. Uncle motioned to Bob, "Come on—let's hope for the best. I'll get word in the morning how he's doing. Get some rest. Yeah, tomorrow's another day. I'm sure his butcher and his sales gal will be minding the store. Don't know if they'll close it for a while. I doubt it though. As they say, the show must go on."

Bob awoke to the smell of scrambled eggs mixed with Uncle's favorite sauce—a blend of herbs

and spices he claimed was a secret recipe from his grandmother.

Aunty doubted these claims, but Uncle stuck to his story. Anyway, the smell wafted upstairs through the vent system and tickled his palate.

Sitting upright in bed, his first thought was he hoped Dan would pull through that horrific fire. His second thought was why did the fire have to start in the first place? He was glad his wife and children were away at the time. They most certainly now would be at the hospital, probably there in Traverse City by his bedside praying for a miracle.

Today, for Bob, was no special day. But how many worries could he think about at one time. He was worried about Daniel possibly being at that shed around the time Morris Tanner was killed.

Why couldn't he just go to the store, purchase the items on his list, and take them home? What did Uncle always tell him—curiosity killed the cat. He was always worried that the McChesney family might have something to do with the Tanner death and Uncle's property was very close to the McChesney property; hopefully they didn't overlap.

Bob was worried. Did he measure the property counting every step with his size twelve shoe? And what about those inventions and drawings? How much were they worth? Were they worth enough for someone to be killed? Bob thought it was a good thing they were in police custody. But what did Uncle say;

possession was nine-tenths of the law. They were all on Uncle's property as Uncle paid for this land.

What was Uncle thinking about all this. And would the McChesney family or someone else try to lay claim to these items? Uncle told Bob there may be people "coming out of the woodwork" to claim these machines and the drawings, even the tools from the shed. He was also fearful for the migrants as some people disliked them for a variety of reasons. He was especially concerned for the Ortez family and his close friend Daniel. He liked their traditions and their close-knit family.

So on this day, when he had little to do, there was so much to think about.

The smell was getting stronger. Breakfast awaited. The news of Dan would come soon enough this morning. One more thing to worry about . . . .

Bob finished his breakfast, and Uncle took him to a room. Was it Uncle's den, Aunty's sewing room, or just a place where a large Hammond organ was residing, which nobody ever played.

"Sit down, Bob. Yes, on that bench. I'm tellin' you, Dan has succumbed—big word, eh—to too much smoke. He passed on an hour or so ago. He was the strength of our community. Of all the people in our place, he was the best.

"Oh Bob, what can I tell you. I can cry. You can cry. What is this life we are given? We live; we die. Dan should have had many more years of life to give us our "daily bread." He was an inventor. He thought he knew how to rewire his home. This was an electrical fire to be sure. All I can say Bob is we're going to have a "wake," a get-together at Persons Harbor next week along with the annual craft fair. I've told your mom to let you stay up here with Aunty and I; we will honor Dan."

The tears streamed from Bob's face. "But why, Uncle? Why is this happening? He was my friend for many years. He let me behind his counter. I saw the meats he was selling. I went into his freezer. What is it to be dead anyway?"

Uncle spoke: "We all don't know when we will leave this earth. Your aunty and I have been fortunate to be together for over fifty years. Our life is not easy. With that new home we are building we're heading toward a new beginning. Aunty has health problems. I'm not as young as I used to be. You are growin' up. Each moment a new beginning. Let's pay our respects to Dan. I've known him for a long time. Let's cherish his memory. Aunty and the other ladies of the club are preparing a celebration for Dan and our successes, trying to make this livin' a success.

"And we love the migrants tryin' to eke out a livin' in these parts, some callin' it the Northern Woods. But next to that Big Lake out there . . . well, we'll have that fillet at the get-together. The ladies makin' little clothes for the migrants' newborn babies. And we'll keep up the education for those migrants. Keep Daniel as your friend, Bob."

Bob took this all in. He would look forward to the get-together, the "wake," next week at Persons Harbor. He was glad to be able to stay an extra week with his aunt and uncle. He would miss Dan—so many emotions came flooding into his being at one time.

This was the "high season" for cherries. His aunt would be

making pies, tarts, cookies, adding to the jampot, all from cherries.

Bob would be able to stay for these festivities. And whatever he thought a community to be, everyone he knew would be at Persons Harbor to remember Dan and to celebrate the annual craft fair. This celebration was beginning to be a tradition. The Great War was in the rear-view mirror of the citizens. This small community was getting larger. People were coming here to enjoy the vacation atmosphere.

Now, Bob slipped under the covers. He prayed his friend Dan was at peace. For the next few days, he would take it easy. There were still many questions unanswered, which bothered him. He hoped Daniel was not a suspect in the murder of Mr. Tanner anymore. He also wondered if the McChesney family was as mean as Uncle had said they were. And now to think about, what were his aunt's health problems? And were there any new clues as to who might have killed Mr. Tanner?

He would pass the next few days before the fair watching Janina doing her diving; maybe he would run into Heather. He could do some fishing by the bridge. The rainbows were running now.

He could always go to the marina and clean the Lyman Islander. Perhaps, too, he could help Aunty with some chores around The Big House.

There would be one more trip to the dump before the fair. Didn't Uncle say the resorts' shoreline needed work. *Build up the breaker wall*, Uncle said. One of the cottages needed painting. Now that would be a "big job for a growing young man like you, Bob." Was his uncle kidding when he spoke to Bob about this project in this way?

Last, the foundation was being started at the new home and sooner than Uncle had expected. He hoped the house would be done by the fall hunting season. He and Aunty planned on staying this year to the end of the firearms hunting season.

Chapter 8.

The Community Unites: An Event at Persons Harbor Craft Fair and a Wake

Bob awoke to the sound of trucks pummeling over the swing bridge. The content on these trucks bore the labor of the region's cherry growers—namely the migrants who spilled their physical exertion, filling crates and crates of this red fruit. The trucks headed to markets in cities around the region. This season was one of the most productive in recent memory.

But for the migrant workers it all was still a financial struggle just to survive the season . . . putting their own food on the table and being able to take care of their own health concerns, let alone their educational problems learning the English language and to read and write in proper English. These seasonal workers still looked for help from the Ladies Auxiliary of Persons Harbor.

Bob hoped the Ortez family would be at the fair and any other migrant laborer. He didn't know if this fair was open to everyone. He hoped it was. As he came downstairs Uncle guided him to the den for what he said was some kind of news concerning the killing of Morris Tanner.

"Bob, there's been some news regarding Morris Tanner's death. There was an escapee from our state's psychiatric hospital about the time of his death. He's been captured and is talking to our sheriff. Whether he's credible or not, I suppose the doctors at the hospital will determine. Also, the sheriff's department is releasing to me those contraptions and those drawings. I've arranged to have them stored in a vault at the Alden State Bank. I'll have to pay for their storage. Aunty isn't too happy. She wants me to donate the items to the local historical society, but I say they may be worth some coin, so I'll just hold on to them a while longer. She's all a tizzy anyway, tomorrow being the first day of the festival. There's some other ladies who are makin' jam and knittin' booties and baby stuff. It's competition don't ya know, blue ribbons at stake and all.

"Then late in the afternoon, it's time to pay respects to Dan. Reverend Cook will preside. A full day to be sure. Today go do your thing; stay outta trouble. Dinner's at five o'clock. Tomorrow I'll be on the grill fixin' up those fillets. You can be with me then; watch a master at work."

Bob spoke up, "Thanks for confiding in me. That's a new word I just learned. I hope all our friends will be at the fair tomorrow."

"And you especially would like Heather there. Am I right? Or maybe you grew a liking for Isabella—more your age. My, my we are getting bigger, hopefully not too big for your britches," said Uncle, his stomach rolling as he laughed uncontrollably. Nephew blushed, "They're just friends. I still like Daniel best."

After breakfast he went outside to walk along a nature trail high on a hillside and was able to look at the majesty of the Big Lake. He thought about the big fish that didn't get away and his experience at the Mexican festival with Daniel, Isabella, and the rest of the Ortez family. And to run into Heather, another friend, that was a coincidence, another big word in his vocabulary.

He hoped Aunty would win a lot of blue ribbons. She worked hard keeping the resort going and volunteering at the clubhouse. Life was good except he wanted to know who killed Morris Tanner and why.

He knew the McChesney family would be at the fair and Uncle told him to be polite—just mingle a little. Stay close to Uncle as Aunty would be busy with the competitions and "other activities."

"Help me unload my goodies," Aunty directed Bob. Uncle moved the truck to a spot outdoors in the back of the building.

There were long tables set up to accommodate the many craft projects to be judged. Another area was set aside for the public to bring their plates of food to enjoy some time during the afternoon activities. Farther back on an incline was a dais where the speakers would call out the contestant's names—the winners and runner-ups. Other notables would give brief remarks, thanking the Persons Harbor Ladies Auxiliary club for hosting the event.

Inside the clubhouse there would be demonstrations of various knitting, quilting, and sewing techniques. Aunty displayed her own unique style, especially creating little bonnets and bowties for newborn babies. She also donated many summer runners for the many tables outside. Aunty later in the day would present Reverend Cook, of the local non-denominational church, to the audience to provide a brief prayer and tribute to Dan Way and his family on his tragic passing. A regular funeral service would be

held later in the week at the Reverend's church.

Bob noticed Uncle was now busy with some friends; "friendly competitors" he called them in the real estate business. He knew when Uncle stoked his pipe he would be discussing this resort business with his friends for a while. Bob drifted away, having met Aunty's directives, nothing more to be set up. He began to wander up one side of a table and down the other which were filled with crafts, most of which did not interest him.

The subjects ranged from woodcarving to salt shakers to clock collections, none of which held his interest. But then he came to a table displaying drawings of what he thought were strange objects. The title of this display—Moving Forward: Prototype Sketches and Devices of a New World to Come. There was one, a strange-looking creature, all metal, in which the arms were moving, and each leg moved up and down. From its mouth a voice was heard to speak: "My name is Rolo the Robot. I am a manmade creature. See I can move my arms and legs." This was repeated over and over.

Next to this creature was a small metal dog with a voice box similar to the robot. It made a barking noise over and over; rather annoying Bob thought.

"I see you've noticed my exhibit," said a voice over Bob's shoulder. "What do you think about it?"

"I think it's interesting . . . different than the lady craft exhibits I passed by. You have a machine here, arms and legs moving and some voice box talking. Interesting."

"Oh, my name is Cecil McChesney by the way—inventor, entrepreneur, financier. And you, I know, are Uncle's nephew. Your name please?"

"Bob. So you are an inventor." Bob was interested yet cautious.

"Yes, the future of mankind is upon us. After the war, we have the opportunity to make great changes in our civilization. We are all consumers. We need products and services, new ways to make our lives easier and more productive. You noticed here Rolo. So, what can a robot do? Wash your car, clean your house, take the place of workers on an assembly line. Out here in the North Woods, pick our fruit. Yes, it will put people out of work, but every generation needs to find other ways to work, carry their load, make a living . . . ." Cecil's eyes lit up, brow upturned, his face contorted almost nastily. It made Bob squeamish; his stomach turned.

"So, these machines will put people out of work," Bob remarked.

"Don't look so sad, my friend. It's just the price of doing business." Cecil's face displayed an arrogance, a defiant nature. "And don't think I don't know your uncle has those machines and plans. Where are they, my man?"

Bob, wanting to get away from this strange character, only remarked: "I don't know what you are talking about."

He moved quickly to other tables. Now he only desired to view the crafts the auxiliary ladies put out. He spotted Uncle beginning to grill the lake trout fillets, and he moved quickly by him.

"Well, just in time Nephew, er, Bob. Time to feed the crowd." Uncle was all smiles, the many pounds of fillet waiting for the grill master to make his move.

"Okay, just sidle up young'un and watch the master at work. I

already put together the ingredients for the glaze over the fillets. (see recipe back of book)

"Each fillet gets a two-minute treatment on each side. The dressing gets poured on over the hot fillet after four minutes. We've got forty pounds of fillet here. We'll keep the line moving. Stay at the end of the grill. Put a finished piece of fillet on each plate as our customers pass by in the line.

No talking, just workin' in rhythm." Uncle was now totally focused on the job at hand. Bob complied and the assembly line process continued until all the fillet pieces were grilled and placed on the plates of the fairgoers. Other volunteers along this assembly line process handed out hot grilled vegetables and grilled potatoes in foil wrap.

Most of the fairgoers were treated to the best fillet they ever ate. One of the food critics from a local newspaper claimed the fillets to be a "feast for the eyes—a palate savoring gourmet meal for the soul."

Bob met many of his friends as they, plate in hand, made their way down the line; he fitting a piece of fillet neatly on each dish as they passed in procession.

Heather stopped for a moment to ask if Bob could meet her at the awards ceremony later in the afternoon. She would be by the dais.

Bob peeked up from his duties and stood eye to eye with Heather—noticing her freckles, curls falling off her shoulders, eager smile, white teeth perfectly positioned—and could only utter, "Yes, I'll look for you. I'll be there."

The awards ceremony was about to begin. The crowd had been fed, and the craft items in several categories had been judged. The awards were about ready to be presented. Aunty guided Reverend Clifford Cook to the podium where he would give a few remarks on behalf of the Way family and the tragedy that befell them.

Bob found Heather among the throng of fairgoers. Everyone who was up for an award squeezed to the front of the crowd.

"And the award for best jam of the season goes to Ms. Ivy Two Shoes." Aunty winced at this pronouncement, Ivy Two Shoes. She was what was called a Native American, living here for a few years in the area. What was it about her jam that was so special?

Aunty thought again that she submitted entries in the scone category, the biscuit category, and the muffin category as well as the pure jelly category, and she failed to even place in any of those areas—a disappointing day to say the least.

Oh well, she thought, Uncle was up for the glaze topping award.

"And the winner of the glaze topping is—Uncle, known as the grill master of the North Woods."

There was wild applause from the crowd. Uncle's pipe dropped from his mouth, now lost forever, but his face lit up, eyes aglow, gripping the trophy like a school kid just defeating a bully in a backyard brawl.

No words were spoken. He glanced over at Aunty, shrugged his shoulders, smiled, and returned to his chair near the dais.

Bob, sitting next to Heather, followed Uncle's path back to his seat. Uncle turned and noticed Heather smiling at Bob and squeezing his hand. Bob's attention was distracted as Aunty introduced Reverend Cook. The day's activities were coming to a close.

The Big Lake had calmed down. It's many speckled hues of purple and blue put a capstone on the day's activities. The community had come together again to provide every citizen with an opportunity to participate in an annual event, which after these few years now perhaps could be considered a tradition.

"May I say we are gathered here in the sight of the Creator by the Big Lake in this warm early summer day to once again remind ourselves we are all blessed to be sharing this communal spirit—each of us participating in our own way helping each other understand what true brotherhood is all about. I want to extend my deepest sympathy to the Way family, Dan being an integral and important member of our fledgling community.

"He treated all of us as equals. He shared his entrepreneurial spirit and expertise with all of us, especially those struggling in their own homes and communities making ends meet—especially nourishing food. I understand this fillet today of lake trout was prepared by one of Dan's butchers and grilled by the award-winning Uncle. Again, let us pray we can continue these festivities for years to come. Blessed be the Lord." The Lord's Prayer followed with an Amen.

Aunty found Uncle, and Bob parted ways with Heather. She told him to come down to their cottage this next weekend, right before Bob was to depart for home downstate.

"Okay, I think Uncle and Aunty are planning on visiting your parents. It'll be some resort business and some just a get-together." Bob started to find Uncle and Aunty as Heather squeezed his hand. Bob's heart beat rapidly. He blushed and spotted Uncle's truck.

He had some questions to ask Uncle about this Cecil character. The killer was still "at large," a term he heard a detective say a week before going with Uncle to the county sheriff's office.

Uncle would be happy with his trophy. What would Aunty say about not winning any trophies or ribbons? But this was a long day for everyone. Now Bob had only a few more vacation days left.

Day after tomorrow he would go to Traverse City with Uncle in an attempt to save the Crystal Inn. What that was all about only Uncle knew. But maybe on the way both could discuss what this vacation trip meant to Bob. He wanted, too, to ask questions about the death of Morris Tanner, and now the new house was under construction on the property Bob marked off.

He looked forward to a good night's sleep. This vacation turned out to be very satisfying, yet troubling at the same time. How that could be . . . maybe his uncle had some of the answers. He couldn't wait to find out.

And the Big Lake was always there, ever present its history going back ages. Many mysteries, yet many charming stories his uncle brought up from time to time. But how could a big body of water reveal to humans what life was all about—we who are human.

"Now I lay me down to sleep" . . . another day in the North Woods to reveal itself.

Chapter 9.
A Trip to Traverse to Save the Inn

At breakfast the next morning, Uncle kept using a new word Bob had not heard before—hemorrhage. *Yes, that inn is hemorrhaging. Just losing money. How can those yokels run a business; so much promise and lose money. Is someone pilfering funds?*

"Well, Bob, we've gotta go to Traverse. We'll meet with those lawyers there—I got one of my own and we'll figure this thing out."

Bob felt as if Uncle was including him in the decision making even though Uncle kept talking to himself.

The trip was less than a thirty-minute drive, so Bob felt compelled to begin asking questions as soon as they headed past the Kewadin sign toward the main highway then a few miles north to the highway, which ran along the bay into Traverse. Their destination was the Park Place Hotel, an old hotel that served as a landmark for the city and its culture.

Everyone who traveled to Traverse had heard of the Park Place. This week was the beginning of the annual cherry festival in the region. There would be much activity at the hotel.

Bob would busy himself just gazing at the ensemble of characters gathered there and maybe would be witness to the many groups representing the festival just beginning to move into the hotel.

"Ah, I don't know what the problems are with that inn. Old man Whitcomb my lawyer told me to attend this meeting at noon. Maybe our group can bail this inn out, give it some leverage, some funds to keep it on its feet. I hear the toads who are running it are skimming money off the top, driving it into bankruptcy."

Every weekend those twenty-four rooms are rented out. They can charge a king's ransom and still have those rooms rented out. And with that sandbar as a beach, it's the angels' playground.

"Oh, Bob, sorry. I see you have some things on your mind to discuss," said Uncle, turning toward Bob and patting the back of his head.

"I met a strange man at the fair, Uncle—the one with the robot. That was Cecil, Mr. McChesney's brother. He says robots are our future. He claims to be an inventor. Oh, and he knows you have those 'contraptions' and all those plans and maps Morris Tanner owned.

"He almost came real close to my face and yelled at me to tell him where those machines and plans were located. It scared me. Inside I got mad. If he touched me, Uncle, I think I would have hit him." Bob's face grimaced.

"Calm down, Bob. One step at a time. We know Cecil and Morris were competitors. They argued over whatever prototypes they were working on. Maybe Cecil was at that shack where Morris was killed either before, during, or after the murder. So far Cecil may be a person of interest, but not a suspect.

"The rest of the McChesney family may be suspects, but that is yet to be proven. We've secured all the contraptions and plans in a vault at the Alden State Bank. Let's just enjoy the day. I'll do my thing; you can wander around the hotel, have a lunch, look at the pretty queens. I shouldn't be long. Either our group gets involved with the inn or we don't."

As the conversation ended, the truck pulled into the hotel's parking lot. Uncle went into a conference room. Bob took a seat in the main dining room as a waiter came over to take his lunch order. He observed many people bustling throughout the hotel. The queens were outside on a veranda. He was enjoying this time with his uncle. He felt free to see all that was going on around him. Maybe Uncle would share in the ownership of the inn, maybe not. At any rate just to spend this business day with him was enough of a pleasure for Bob. He ordered from the adult menu. He would sit and observe this day's events. Cherries were a very important crop to harvest. To have a festival named after a fruit, he thought, was very important for the region. Many people and groups made their living existing from this fruit. He wondered if Daniel, his family, and all the migrants felt this same way. After-all, they were the most important group getting the fruit picked, the first step in the harvesting process.

But then what was that contraption all about which would jiggle the fruit off the trees? Were these machines designed to put the migrants out of business? So many questions. Bob finished his meal just as Uncle came out of the conference room with news about the inn.

Uncle strolled toward Bob's table. "Well did you feast your eyes on the lovely ladies here at the festival? Really the pre-festival. Oh, Aunty and I are skipping the main week this year . . . too many tourists in the area. Never thought I'd live to utter these words."

He stopped to re-light his pipe. "This dang new pipe doesn't have the ventilation the old one I lost had."

Bob spoke up: "So what's the news on the inn. Did you step in and save it? I mean you and the other investors?" He wanted to sound business-like, this trip being about business.

"No, we couldn't pull the trigger on any deal. Too many details to overcome. We did look at their books, however, found some shoddy work practices. You know, Bob, we want these owners to succeed. What's good for the goose is good for the gander."

This saying confused Bob, but he nodded as if he knew what Uncle meant. Uncle went on: "You know we just had to show them how to balance their books, income, outgo. Boring stuff you might say, but necessary to run a business.

"Darn pipe—now it's clogged with tobacco that won't burn." Uncle became distracted.

"Thanks for telling me about your business. It seems it's hard to get started; then there are those bills you have to pay every month. I don't know how you and Aunty do it. And the new house you are building up the road. Thanks for letting me mark it off. I'm glad I was born with and grew such big feet." Both laughed at Bob's sense of humor.

"Well, let's head on out. Get back home. Wonder what Aunty has for dinner? I'm still full from those lake trout fillets," said Uncle, looking down at his belt buckle. "Yes sir, I had to move out two notches after all that food at the fair."

As soon as the two entered the back door of the house, Aunty came rushing up to Uncle.

"Some kind of emergency at the Alden State Bank," she said. "Give Sam Creedon, their president, a call."

"Don't I get a hug first? I've been sweating bullets in Traverse with that inn deal; fell through. Though we came to some agreement about how they should do business."

Aunty ushered Uncle to the den, the main business room in the house. "Get on the phone now before you eat and are too tired to call after dinner."

"I'm dialing, I'm dialing. Hello, yeah, put me through to Sam. Tell him it's the Northwind calling. No, no kidding. Sounds horrible. Yeah, I'm mad. You can't secure your own bank. What am I supposed to do now? Insurance. No, I had no need, I thought, for insurance; not when items are in a bank vault. I thought they'd be secure. Okay, okay. I'll be over to sign some paperwork tomorrow. So, you've turned in a report to the police. Yes, that's the first step. You say what? Ed Sneeds gone missing? Your VP sounds like you've got some explaining to do. All right, see you first thing in the morning." Uncle hung up the phone.

Aunty, standing in the hallway, faced Uncle. "Well, what's up? Sounds like bad news. I knew it was urgent."

"Well, where do I start. It seems everything I took over to the bank has gone missing, along with their VP, vanished into thin air. Probably broke in last night. Cleaned out everything . . . the contraptions, all the plans and drawings. He's on the lam. For cryin' out loud how far does he expect to get with all that stuff?"

"I told you," Aunty now turning a crimson color, face contorted in a frown and anger beginning to erupt. "Give that stuff to the local historical society. Let them take the responsibility and heat. But no. You had to keep it. You thought it was worth some money. You and money . . . always a scheme. I said we'd build a business, slow and steady, but you had to blaze a fast trail in this resort business. Get ahead of the pack you always said. Be the first to have four cottages, all brick and masonry, not tinderbox cabins. Be the first to have two-bedroom cottages, good indoor plumbing, propane gas, on the lake. Oh, and you had to buy that big fishing boat, show it off, take friends and foe alike on long excursions on the lake, always burning up precious fuel. And then you had to buy, at the very beginning of our time up here, this big home, five bedrooms. You've invited everyone here to enjoy themselves, not charging anyone a dime, even second cousins we don't even know. And I know you and Dan Way had schemes to help people—a lot of those migrants have enough food to eat now and you took several of them fishing in Round Lake—showed 'em where the hittin' spots were located where they caught the best catches in the area whenever they went out. A noble attitude you have if we could ever afford it. And now this business; that Tanner character dead; now the bank VP takin' all that stuff; gone missin'," tears rolling down Aunty's cheek.

Bob, a safe distance behind Aunty, never heard these arguments before. Once in a while he tuned in to discussions when he was in bed upstairs, listening through the air vent. But now this turn of events, a term Uncle would be familiar with, was taking place in this once tranquil place. Everything now unraveled at once.

Uncle spoke up: "Okay, Aunty, enough of this wrangling. I'll go over to the bank tomorrow, see what I have to do and report all that stuff missing. Remember, we got a barbecue to go to at the

Junkers; a lot of people will be there. You've got just two days left, Bob. Our problems are our problems. No sense involving my favorite nephew. Let's just sleep on it. Tomorrow will bring its own set of problems. And we've got all the cottages rented for the weekend. Boy, they sure are gainin' ground on our new home. The foundation is set. The framing will be up in a week or so. You'll have your breezeway in this home Aunty. Plenty to be joyful for. I'm glad we all agreed today to help those folks running the Crystal Inn. We're all in this business together."

There was no chocolate sundae this evening. Bob thought a minute as he looked across the lake at the lights at the Alden baseball field. He and Uncle never made it over to the park this trip. He also realized this would be the last of two nights sleeping in the Big House. He knew every inch of the place and now with future visits would learn where his room would be located in the new home. Uncle told him the new home would be on just one floor. He said it was a ranch style, whatever that meant.

His thoughts now turned to Heather who would be at the barbecue the following day. For him it would mean his last full day here with his uncle and aunt in these North Woods.

Chapter 10.

Life's Lessons Learned Well—
Bob's Soul to Keep in the North Woods

Breakfast the next morning was quiet. "Eat all your Wheaties, Bob, and the banana. Must have your potassium, don't you know." His aunt encouraged him with every spoonful.

"I can smell a different flavor of berry in the jampot—you must be melting in another type of fruit," said Bob, slowing his eating a bit.

"Oh, you notice. Yes, the blackberries are in season. Some say they don't smell, but they do when mixed with other fruit."

"Uncle must be at the bank in Alden. He left early." Bob swallowed the last spoonful of cereal.

"Yes, he called a while ago. You were still catching your *ZZZs*. He'll be back soon. This afternoon we're going to the Macky's place at the point. Actually, now it's just Juliana Macky since her husband passed away last fall. Seems all the area's business people will be there. She's been a force with the businesses around the region. You know her place; we call it the Chalet. I suspect the Junkers will be there. Those two sisters you know. I guess Janina will miss her four o'clock jump today." Aunty moved around the kitchen putting dishes and silverware away.

Uncle's truck sputtered out back in the driveway. He entered the back door, the screen door slamming shut.

"Take it easy, old man. Sit down. Cool off. You look like you've just hiked up the Matterhorn and breathed your last breath," Aunty said, motioning to Uncle to calm down.

"Those bank people give me the willies. All those contraptions gone, the papers gone, the drawings gone. Right out of the vault. And worst of all their big cheese Ed Sneed gone—disappeared. Can't find hide nor hair of his carcass. Then, I was told sign this release form; sign that form. I'm not signing squat. It's their fault. I told 'em I've got my lawyer workin' to sue you boys. They told me they had their lawyer working to partially relieve them of liability. They told me to file a claim with my homeowner's insurance. And on and on we went.

"They said that since I didn't put an amount of worth on the items, they'll pay out just one hundred dollars. So sue us, they said. The sheriff was there and took my statement and will file a report for stolen property. Good luck, he said, on ever getting it back.

"This will be the talk of the party this afternoon. Word gets around faster than Lone Ranger's speeding bullet. I got to sit a spell; wash up later. Get ready to go smooch up to Juliana."

Bob took these moments of concern to heart. There was so much happening. He was having problems piecing all the parts together.

"You can go out and play ball. Catch some crickets and grasshoppers for the bug box. You can make yourself useful by taking the hand mower and mowing that patch of grass growing wild behind the shed." Aunty hinted at Bob to stay away from Uncle's wrath for a while.

"Okay, I'll make myself useful." He took the hint and went

outside to put his physical self to work. He thought, if time permits, he could even straighten up the shed a bit. There was the smell of rotting fish; Uncle used the word "putrid." He would mix some cleaning solution with hot water and would scrub the floor, work benches, and other areas in the shed that Uncle said were "putrid."

After these chores were done, Bob, Uncle, and Aunty cleaned up, put on clean party clothes, and headed for Uncle's vintage super '98 Oldsmobile. He had it restored two years ago. It was, he said, a showpiece. He would make a fine entrance to the barbecue with these "wheels."

Aunty reminded Bob to bring his bathing suit, big beach towel, and number seventy suntan lotion. The grandchildren, nieces, and nephews would be swimming along the Macky's beachfront. One of her grandchildren may set sail and, with today's wind, could get up to twenty knots on the open water.

Upon arrival Bob was greeted by Amelia Junker, Heather's Mom. She pointed out to a large raft anchored some fifty yards offshore at this part of deepwater point, a drop-off of over fifty feet.

"I know you can swim out to that raft. Heather told me to tell you to meet her out there," Amelia kept on pointing. Bob's trunks were under his jean pants. He quickly disrobed and began his swim in the icy water. When he arrived at the raft he held on to the ladder and hoisted himself on to the raft, which bobbed with the movement of the waves.

His first view of Heather found her face down on her stomach, the sun scorching her back. Her bikini was loosely-fitted on her torso. She was wearing the latest fashion sunglasses. Her tousled blond hair formed a mane down her back.

"Well, as I live and breath will miracles never cease. I made it out here by boat; you stroked your way onto my island home. Just don't stand on the ladder, come over and keep me from burning up; number seventy lotion if you please—start with the neck and move on down."

Bob gulped as he found his bearings on this wobbly raft. He took a minute to view the vast expanse of the lake—today it was assured every known factor leading to perfection. This moment to remember was in place and Heather urged him to join her, this place, this time. He felt delirious, or maybe just a nauseous sensation, out of breath from the swim to this island paradise. He complied. The lotion mixed in with the sweat and airy sea breeze on Heather's body.

"Now finish the job. Along the ankles please." She awakened Bob's senses as he came out of a stupor still trying to acclimate to the rolling, pitching, and yawing of this raft. Heather now propped her body on her left elbow, her head turned toward Bob, face to face.

Bob spoke: "So, I'm out of breath. Let me catch it. Isn't the lake sparkling?" He thought that comment to be a revelation.

Heather spoke again picking up the pace. "So those were your fillets at the fair, yours and your uncle's. You caught that monster way out there," she said, pointing to a spot between Deepwater and French Point. "Way to go. So this trip has been fun for you. I know you like or appreciate my sister's diving skills. I could never do that—too risky. I hope you'll stay for the fire pit get-together. I'll eat a marshmallow you roast for me. I'm not much on those bigshot people comin' here. My mom and dad think it's

important to be around people who invest in this "resort" business, Mrs. Macky being the big cheese." Heather's tone became serious.

Bob jumped in: "Do you like your marshmallow somewhat charred or just plain warm and mushy?"

Heather laughed. "You have a way with words. Yes, charred is in. With your decisions I'm livin' in the fast lane. Oh, I see my younger bro' comin' to pick me up—his putt putt Evinrude. Are you up to the challenge? Beat him to the beach. Stroke all the way."

"Okay, I'm game." Bob stood up, regained his footing, and dove into the icy water to begin the crawl to shore.

As he reached the beach, he heard the Evinrude conk out. Heather came toward Bob placing her hand on his hand raising it in victory: "And the winner by an eyelash—my hero Bob!"

As the evening wore on, Bob noticed his aunt and uncle participating in many animated conversations. Apparently, this get-together was very important. There was Janina getting involved in some of the meetings. He concluded this get-together was for people who had money, wanted money, or who needed some backing for their ventures.

The migrant families were not here. What was his friend Daniel up to this beautiful, starry night. Probably exhausted and resting, sleeping after a week of picking fruit, namely cherries, as this season was beginning to be the most important of all for the growers of the area.

As his mind wandered, remembering the time spent with his

uncle these past few weeks, he breathed easily. His uncle confided in him about the secrets he revealed. Yes, they were a team.

Did the people here this evening catch up on the news that Uncle's contraptions, plans, and diagrams were stolen . . . an inside job from the Alden Bank? He didn't hear anyone mention this event. He did hear some congratulate Uncle on breaking new ground for his and Aunty's new home. And selling those cottages at market value was a good deal to be sure.

"I said I like my marshmallows slightly charred. You burned them to a crisp." Heather now sat next to Bob.

He had been distracted by his own thoughts. This marshmallow was not really meant for Heather. "Oh, sorry. Let me get another one on a stick for you. Tell me when."

"When." Bob extended the stick toward Heather's mouth. One gulp.

"Now, let me roast one for you. Let me know when."

The marshmallow took on a yellowish glow. After a few seconds Bob spoke up: "Enough."

Heather reached over to place the marshmallow in his mouth. Some of the goo dribbled down onto his jaw. Both laughed.

The noise from the evening's activities subsided. The fire died down, but the embers remained.

The stars twinkled in the sky. Tonight, many galaxies were glowing over the Big Lake.

"Come on, Nephew, er, Bob." Uncle broke the silence between Heather and Bob, both of whom were consumed with thoughts of their own, yet this evening were the consummate

couple—innocent in their understanding of the bigger world of finance and adult intrigue . . . just two people coming together to share each other's trivial pursuits, caring for each other's feelings, but naïve as to how the adult world works.

Heather, the investigator, advanced in the biological process moving more into her teen years facing those perceived challenges and fears. Bob, the follower, knowing these moments of joy and innocence would not last, stood at a moment in time—body and soul nourished this day, but unknowing as to what his future would bring.

"So, write to me. Here is my address. I enjoyed this day," she said, following Bob to the car.

"I enjoyed it, too. It seemed to go all too fast." Bob got into the car.

Heather reached over and kissed Bob on his forehead. Aunty and Uncle giggled; both together uttered "puppy love."

"This was a time well spent; many contacts to put in our rolodex." Uncle beamed at Aunty.

Bob was left with his thoughts. Yes, a day well spent as his head turned back toward Heather. He caught a glimpse of her smile. He tucked her address into his pants pocket. Another summer vacation for Bob winding down, but a new beginning of feelings and possibilities for Bob as he, tomorrow, would go back to his old world of day-to-day routines and daily strife.

"Goodbye, Heather. I know we have much to experience in the days, weeks, and months ahead."

"Off to bed now, Bob. Your parents will be here mid-afternoon tomorrow." Uncle ushered him upstairs to the bedroom in the front with a view of the Big Lake. This was the last night for Bob in the room, his last night in this house. The new house was moving along and would soon be complete.

The scream, more of an angry roar, came early in the morning at sunrise from the shed in back of the house.

"This is a horrible mess. I thought Bob cleaned it out yesterday." Tools were everywhere, a bench overturned, the cabinets broken into—a total disaster. Aunty was furious but calmed down a bit.

"Someone broke in here; the lock is broken. It couldn't be an animal. No animal rifles through drawers and cabinets."

Uncle beat a path to the shed: "What on earth are you—" he stopped mid-sentence, surveying the damage. With a forlorn look on his face spoke slowly: "Well, I'll be a monkey's uncle. Someone's been here in the middle of the night. No rascal animal could be this organized—lookin' into drawers and such."

Aunty confronted Uncle: "Do you know anything about this? You did take all those contraptions and plans outta here, didn't you? Now they're gone. Good riddance, I say."

"No, girlie, I don't know what this is all about. Seems some random act of neighborhood vandalism—that's what it must be." Uncle examined the damage.

"At least I still got my expensive fishing poles, and my fillet knives are all here. Just a random break in," he repeated to himself.

Bob packed his belongings. Aunty had washed his clothes earlier in the week. She packed some of her oatmeal raisin cookies and jampot jam in a separate container and told Bob to share them with his parents and siblings.

There was Kodak moment photo prints of Bob and other friends of the family who were together during this visit. The one Bob would cherish the most—he and Uncle at the marina next to the big lake trout caught in the Big Lake.

Aunty also gave him a picture of him and Dan taken in the market during the first day of this trip. Then there were pictures of Isabella's coming out party. He especially like the picture of himself and Daniel—arms around each other, Heather waving toward the camera in the background.

Just an hour or so before his parents were to arrive, Uncle called Bob into the den. He sat him down and then sat next to him.

"I've got a confession to make. You and I have been square with each other. There's a lot to think about for you and me. We've been doing some detective work, but there's one more item I've got to get off my chest. I wasn't completely honest with Aunty earlier about not knowing what the break in of the shed was all about. I've got one more map and a deed I can't figure out; kept them pieces of paper close to me. Seems there's a gravel pit around here. It's just been dug out a few years ago, so it seems, and abandoned. It contains pelitic rocks, clay, and calcite. Seems it's very valuable. All this rock is used in the manufacturing of cement. Also, the pit may contain specs of gold according to the information on the map.

I've got a deed and directions to the site. Seems the crew over at the Alden State Bank met with Morris Tanner about all this. So, really, I suppose that was another reason Ed Sneed possibly did Morris in.

Maybe it was Ed, snooping around here, who broke into the shed overnight.

I gotta come clean with Aunty about all this and I gotta figure out if the deed and map are real and who I can trust to give me some straight answers.

I got this pit located somewhere in back of Ross' place at the Landing and around up the road to that migrant village. I'll bet the pit is all covered up, but it once was discovered and worked on.

I'm also sure there are others in the community who know about the pit and are lookin' to cash in," said Uncle, now a little out of breath.

"Thanks for filling me in and thanks for the good times I had this time up. I'll have a lot to tell Mom and Dad."

"Oh, but let's keep this pit business just between you and me at least until I figure out my next move." Uncle smiled as rings of smoke came spiraling out of his pipe.

They both reached to hug each other at the same time. Uncle chuckled and spoke, "I think Aunty's gourmet meals have caused a protrusion around your waistline. You'll find you can't run as fast around the bases lest you drop a few pounds."

"And thanks, Uncle, for letting me steer the boat, er, Lyman Islander. We sure did catch a whale of a trout from the Big Lake."

Just then Aunty entered the den. "So, what's all this chattering about? I'm surprised you two don't have a blood pact what with all your time spent together. We're going to miss you, Bob.

This time up you were very helpful what with your cleaning up the cottages and all. You even were able to unscrew a pickle jar for Aunty. You're gettin' bigger and stronger each visit. Oh, this fall Uncle and I are staying up here . . . gonna have Thanksgiving at our new place. Big crowd of people coming to see our new home. I suspect your mom and dad and brother and sister will be makin' the trip. It'll be late fall. May be cold up here, so dress warmly," Aunty added, smiling at Bob.

"Oh, Aunty always the caregiver. Let his mom figure out what he should wear then," said Uncle, chuckling and embracing Bob again.

Just then they heard the sound of a car pulling in the driveway behind the home. Aunty chimed in, "Bob, get out there. Your mom and dad aren't staying. They're picking you on the run."

His mom and dad stopped the car, got out for an instant, exchanged pleasantries with Uncle and Aunty, and motioned for Bob to scoot into the back seat; the luggage was put away in the trunk.

Uncle came over, embraced Bob one more time, and whispered in his ear: "Remember our secrets. We did work together as detectives didn't we, but there is much to find out isn't there. You'll be back here for Thanksgiving. We'll have a big festival. Be sure to ask for the wishbone. I'll get one of those hefty local turkeys from the Simmons farm, save you the big drumstick. You think Aunty's jams are tasty—wait till you taste her bread pudding."

"Okay, okay we're outta here," said his dad, backing the car out to the main road.

His mother, always the inquisitor, asked Bob, "So how did

you like this trip? Do anything new? Anything different?"

"Well, Mom, Dad—Uncle and I caught one of the biggest lake trout this season so far. The fillets fed a lot of people at the fair at Persons Harbor. I met a lot of good people this time. I went to Daniel's sister's coming out party. Uncle let me mark off the property where their new house will be built. Remember my shoe size is twelve." He thought better of telling his parents about the dead body he and Uncle found—too much explaining to do.

"Oh, and my friend Mr. Dan Way died in a house fire. That was a very sad time."

His mother remarked: "Last season Doctor Bond passed away. So, this trip it was Mr. Way in a tragic fire. You're certainly learning what life is all about—it is very precious, son."

Yes, he thought to himself. What is this thing called life all about. So many memories and emotions on this trip. He heard his uncle say Aunty's health was not the best. What was that all about? He hoped Uncle would take care of himself—what with a killer on the loose. And what did those maps locating a gravel pit mean and did Uncle really have the real ownership? Uncle said possession is nine-tenths of the law. But apparently, there were people who would fight for that ownership.

The car, now passing Rapid City, a few small dwellings, a post office, and the remains of a once thriving forestry business turned onto M 72 and started downstate—Bob's adventure in the North Woods complete for another summer.

He hoped this Thanksgiving he would get the long part of the wishbone as he still had plenty of wishes he hoped would come true in the future there in the North Woods . . . for now his soul to keep.

Addendum

Uncle has many sayings, expressions, and ways to express his unique style of conversation. Try and fit some of his sayings into the following categories:

Metaphor—a figure of speech in which a word or phrase is applied to an object or action to which it is not literally applicable. (Ex: Life is a highway.)

Personification—the attribution of a personal nature or human characteristics to something non-human, or the representation of an abstract quality in human form. (Ex: The wing howled in the night.)

Symbolism—the use of symbols to represent ideas or qualities. (Ex: chains-imprisonment; crown-power)

Cliché—an expression once innovative but has lost its novelty due to overuse. (Ex: Play your cards right, better safe than sorry, bring to the table)

Idioms—a group of words established by usage as having a meaning not deducible from those of the individual words. (Ex: rain cats and dogs, see the light)

Metonymy—substitution of the name of an attribute or adjunct for that of the thing meant. (Ex: suit for business executive or the track for horse racing)

Simile—a figure of speech involving the comparison of one thing with another thing of a different kind, used to make a description more emphatic or vivid. (Ex: brave as a lion)

Hyperbole—exaggerated statements or claims not meant to be taken seriously. (Ex: I'm so hungry I could eat a horse. The cold is freezing me to death. She can hear a pin drop. He's as skinny as a rail. They ran like greased lightning. Her brain is the size of a pea. He's got tons of money.)

Uncle created this sauce to place on the lake trout fillet. It was from an old family recipe handed down through the ages by his great-great-grandfather who fished in the 1800s off the Grand Banks.

Lake Trout Fillets

3-5 minutes per side
145 degrees
Panko
grilled potatoes in foil

For every two pounds of fillet:
¼ cup olive oil
1 clove garlic
½ tsp dried sage
½ tsp dried rosemary
2 tbsp wine vinegar
½ tsp salt
¼ tsp black pepper

Combine ingredients and cook over moderate heat till garlic starts to brown (about 2 minutes).

Stir in vinegar, salt and pepper.

Trout fillets in a stainless steel pan.

Sprinkle fish with salt, add oil and vinegar mixture, and turn to coat.

Grill fish skin-side down for 2 minutes.

2 minutes longer—pour remainder over hot fish.

Part II

Bob's Young Soul Continues to Grow in the North Woods

Late fall in this northern clime found most of nature's life dormant. Summer's seasonal events were tucked away in a lockbox of planned, now finished, cycled activities.

The young passenger in a sedan sat in the backseat waiting to arrive at his uncle and aunt's new home.

This time, however, with the air cold, the sky cloudy, and with winds whipping across the Big Lake, the trip seemed out of sequence. School was still in session and everyone talked of turkeys, stuffing, and Aunty's special bread pudding—a time of Thanksgiving.

He noticed the trees, now naked, each tree deciduous with bare skeleton-like branches. The cherry trees, too, lacked fruit this time of year.

The creatures here planned their own retreat with nature showing the way of survival throughout those upcoming bitter cold winter months.

The human population still staying in these North Woods retreated into the warmth of their manmade abodes to "hunker down"—a bunker mentality. Seasonal residents were practically non-existent.

For this youth, in his parent's sedan, the first time to be challenged by the real north Arctic wind—a time of peril.

He was to witness the past era when the Chippewa Indians bade farewell to the splendors of this rich, lush life; when seasons changed from the seeded spring to the seasoned summers and fish and fowl alike provided sustenance—an abundance of food. Nature's scenic view provided their coded physical and psychological well-being—seasons of warmth and beauty.

But now the intrusions—those many seasons past and present, the white patron developer of another kind of manmade despoiler of this pristine environment.

As the sedan drove onto the cement driveway of his aunt and uncle's new home, this youth realized some of the innocence from summer seasons past started draining from his memory.

He was here, out of season. This was a time of Thanksgiving. He was given these days to give thanks for his blessings. Those Pilgrims and Indians came together to worship as a communal time, back in the pre-founding of our country.

But now, he would greet his aunt and uncle in their new home along with many others from the community, many resort owners, to wish them good luck and many more summer seasons of success and happiness.

His parents would stay for Thanksgiving dinner then depart back downstate. His uncle and aunt's son and wife would take Bob back to his home downstate this coming Sunday—this trip seeming to be uneventful.

Would there be anyone coming for the Thanksgiving dinner Bob would know? He didn't know. Just to think in a year or so he would be able to come up to the Big Lake on his own, drive his own car was enough to suggest to him—sitting in the back seat—dad steering—the way someday soon he would be able to travel on his own and escape parental restraints.

He would be on a par with his uncle and aunt in so far as

his ability to suggest certain outcomes for problems; he would help out and would be perceived as an independent nephew who could assume much more responsibility than in previous years coming up to this region of the North Woods, or so he was telling himself. He hoped his uncle would have time on this brief trip to confide in him and inform him if anyone was caught for the murder of Mr. Tanner . . . and if that bank executive was found who stole Uncle's contraptions and drawings? Before he left for the summer, he also remembered Uncle telling him about a map and information maybe leading to a gravel pit somewhere near the migrant village camp. That pit contained a special rock (calcite) for making cement and the pit may contain specs of gold—or so some writings Uncle found supposedly said.

Also, Uncle had a deed to this property. Did that mean the gravel pit belonged to him? Was it legitimate?

He knew his friend Daniel, his family, and the rest of the migrant population went back to their town in Mexico. They would return next spring to begin that season anew.

He wondered if they formed a union to help the many families survive another hard season for them picking fruit and caring for each other's well-being.

"Son, we're here. Did you fall asleep? Get out and help us carry our bags in," said his father, somewhat ruffled from the drive from downstate. There was no stopping this time—not even a potty stop.

Bob made two quick trips, placing the bags in the breezeway of the new home.

Uncle and Aunty were inside tending to guests who had dropped by this Thanksgiving Day. Bob heard the term "cooks tour" referred to by his aunt who was showing guests around this new home.

At the end of the breezeway, the space opened to a large dining room. A long table was already set with proper China and silverware, glasses, and folded napkins. A horn of plenty cornucopia was in the middle of the table. A long runner of browns, oranges, and gold leaf patterns brought out the fall splendor.

Bob's attention was alerted as most of the guests were in the front living room, a large rectangular space with a big bay window through which one could view the Big Lake, now almost colorless with choppy waves crashing on a beach Uncle would later say has public access. A large sign shouted out "Sunrise Terrace." Bob could read this sign clearly from his place entering the living room.

Out of the corner of his eye down the driveway on a spot by the side lawn, he saw large objects hung along a clothesline—but he didn't have time to focus.

"Bob, you're here. Come in, Nephew. Let me take a look at you. It's only been what three, four months—but my how you've grown." The smell of cherry blend filled the air.

His uncle embraced him, enveloping Bob in a bear hug. Aunty, close behind, smiled a bit less demonstrative.

"Welcome to our new home! Let me introduce you to our family."

He recognized Uncle and Aunty's son and daughter-in-law. He would be riding back with them come Sunday. Gene Jolly and his wife stood and shook hands.

Cordy stood up. She was nestled on a bean bag chair. It took much effort to rise.

"Hey, my fourth in canasta. How are you doin'? See you are appropriately dressed for our off season."

"Ya, I'll be headin' to the warmer climes in a week or so but will be back up here next spring for another season as a part-time librarian, part-time volunteer at Persons Harbor, and part-time canasta partner with you, Bob," Candy exclaimed, her voice trailing.

"Nice to meet you all," said Bob. Then he followed Uncle into an adjoining hallway. Uncle spoke, his hand on Bob's shoulder.

"There's a lot you and I are going to talk about. Just go with Aunty's plan. We're all together today for the feast. Friday, I'm goin' to the dump. We'll talk then. No one knows what you and I know. Aunty and I will be goin' south in a few days. I'm in business to sell a new item—motor homes. We'll be there a few months. Then spring will raise its flowered head and we'll be back up here. Friday we'll take a run down Torch River Road to the gravel pit. I know there are others out there who are following what I'm doing. Just go with it. Aunty wants to impress the resort people . . . see the spread she put out," he finished as his voice trailed off.

The trimmings on the ornate table were covered with the amenities of the season. When the Thanksgiving food was placed on the long, mahogany/cherry table, this Thanksgiving was one to eclipse all others.

The Big Lake roared its approval. Howling winds shrieked with pleasure blasting across the lake right into this new residence, causing the wallboards to tremble and the visitors to hesitate and take note that Mother Nature still held her dominant position. She told these seasonal commuters, "You are the fallible fools in my seasonal contrivance. You and your money count for nothing. I laugh at your feebleness to control my temperament. Come to me when you are called, not in this off season of stark weather conditions."

"But today, take note of giving thanks to each other for surviving another season of woe. You do not know what tomorrow will bring—but fight on dear brethren."

The meal was served; conversation limited. "Do you remember, Bob, as a lad, when asked do you like pumpkin or minced meat pie—you said yes, and a slice of each was served to you," Cordy lamented Bob's answer at a Thanksgiving long ago—age five downstate.

"Let's fight for the wishbone. We gave it to Bobby then. We ask what he wished for. Remember he said a teddy bear," Jacqui, Uncle's daughter-in-law, broke in.

Aunty chimed in: "And he named it Bumpy. Served him well when he came up his first year and broke out with chicken pox. Oh, those spots . . . everywhere."

The laughter around the table erupted in a fury of emotion. Bob's face turned a crimson color, and his body slumped, wanting to hide under the immense sanctuary of the table.

Don't these people know I'm a teenager now, not some young kid who didn't know much about what people think, what they plan, what they talk about. At least in the morning I'll be with Uncle. He'll know how smart I am. He'll ask me for advice. We've got a lot to talk about, think about.

"Yes, Aunty, I'll have a sliver of pumpkin and a sliver of

minced meat pie," said Bob, his brow furrowed, and everyone laughed. Tomorrow couldn't come soon enough. He and his uncle had plenty to discuss—important matters.

Arising from his new bed, Bob dressed quickly and walked down a hallway and turned right at the end into the kitchen.

He found his uncle's son and daughter-in-law seated around a large table.

His aunt was busy making pancakes, her jampot preserve in a bowl on the table along with three kinds of syrup. Bacon was crisping in a frying pan. Uncle spoke first: "Well, how did you like sleeping this first night in our new home?"

Bob, rubbing his eyes, a slight stumbling motion when entering this new unfamiliar kitchen, said, "Fine, it'll take a while to get used to just being on one floor."

"Eat up, young'un, er Bob, gotta get to the dump, drop off some no good scrap, then I want to come back—show ya the bucks down by the road—what they're hangin' there for. A couple of experts comin' over to tell me and you all about this deer business. Scraps already on the truck, Bob. Let's leave before anyone's the wiser."

Aunty had scraps from Thanksgiving. No one claimed the carcass this year. Bob had lost in the battle of the wishbone. His uncle's son snapped the bone claiming the bigger half.

Bob thought this tradition to have run its course, he being a teenager—not a whimpering child when the stronger person pulling the bone usually won out and Bobby was left, another year, no wish granted . . . just left with the "short end of the stick"

. . . or so over those many years his uncle bemusing Bob's feeble efforts was left to utter, "Maybe next year young'un."

The trip was short. Bob emptied the truck of its load. "So, let's head back to those bucks—see what our "year round" friends have to report. I've gotta get a lead on the Junkers and Jollys. And the new owners of the Crystal Inn have some plans comin' up next season that'll knock your socks off, Bob."

Standing at one end of a taut clothesline were two men in a deep, studious mode examining one of three large bucks strung up for the public to examine. These were the creatures Bob spotted when he first entered the living room of the new home— now up close they appeared to be mammoth beings, their antlers spreading like large branches of a mature tree whose leaves have fallen and the trunk has a hard time holding these branches up.

"Let me introduce you to our big buck experts. Bob, I'd like you to meet Woody Stencil, Barny's younger brother, and Matt "Boomer" Newsome, cousin to the Jollys."

"Pleased to meet you, Bob. You're uncle here is proud of your boat drivin' skills—we saw the big lake trout you two hooked on to. Didn't have a fightin' chance with you two on the lines," remarked Woody, giving Uncle a wink as Bob took in this group of bucks, his eyes moving down the line—each deer bigger than the previous with their antlers weighing heavily on their heads.

Matt spoke up: "Shall I give Bob here the cooks tour? Okay, I will," he said, not waiting for Uncle to respond.

"These beauts are the result of some mighty precise hunting— lotta prep time, lotta equipment. Bucks here getting bigger and

bigger in these parts. These "old geezers" been around a while.

"Your uncle won the honor to display these creatures. They've been dressed out. Tomorrow they'll head for the butchering process. Plenty of meat on these carcasses," continued Matt.

Woody interrupted Matt's flow: "I'm sure Bob wants to know what these bruts are all about. Remember what I tell ya, son—an education you be gettin'. These here bucks have a lot of drop times—antlers growin' downward far from the deer's head. Observe please. Then there's the brow tine, the first tine that extends forward from the main beam of the antler. Don't look so confused, Bob. Just put your specs on these bucks."

Matt again blurted out—causing Woody to stop chattering—"Then there's the kicker point—a non-typical point that grows out from the burr portion of the antler. Last but not least there's a sticker point, which is a non-typical point branching from one of the typical points. See buck number two a couple of sticker points."

"You got all that, Bob?" Bob's face flushed when his uncle spoke up. "This buck business is new to me." His pipe poured out cherry blend smoke—he was huffing and puffing.

But Woody wasn't through, his gabbing now echoed, an excitement in his voice: "Let me tell ya this third white tail buck had a score of 170, award winning in these parts, in the Midwest, and possibly nationally—excitin' stuff for these North Woods hunters.

"Buck number one is a bad boy. Bucks two and three are bruisers."

Matt again broke in: "That first buck plugged with a Winchester 94; 30-30."

Woody interrupted, "Come on, Matthew; it was a 243 Winchester light recoil. Get it right for once. Bob here deserves to know the name of the weapon."

"Okay, okay," Matt shot back. "I know bucks two and three were plugged through the heart with a Savage 110 bolt action."

Woody finished, "Someone in that first party had a Marlin 336 rifle. I think there were two shots at that buck, both penetrating the heart.

"We still got a lot of work to do to find out what kinda gun was pluggin these rascals—sometimes the bullet goes right through 'em though."

"Okay, okay, 'nuff of this buck education business," said Uncle, wanting to summarize this encounter. "I hope some of the meat goes to the Persons Harbor pantry—to feed those year round residents who struggle during these awful winter months. And maybe someday we'll have a year round season—what with skiing comin' popular; then, too, some machine one hops on and can go through the woods along trails on the snow. Then there's plenty of snow shoeing up here—what with these new trails comin'.

"Year round—maybe in my day, maybe not. But, at any rate, I'm leavin' with the misses; goin' south to sell recreation homes on wheels. Be back next spring. Gotta sell those lots around Deepwater Point. Civilization is advancing at warp speed."

These last few comments were of no interest to Matt and Woody. Their time was done here. They sprinted down the embankment onto the highway—their jeep parked next to a culvert—and off they went.

Uncle and Bob were left standing, looking, admiring, awed

by the bulk of these huge bucks.

Bob thought now was the moment he and Uncle would share catching up, Uncle confiding in Bob.

Uncle's demeanor stiffened then relaxed; an extra puff of cherry blend plumed from his pipe and encircled Bob's head. Now, Bob thought, the real education, this brief trip to be worth the visit would commence.

Uncle came close to Bob. He pulled a stone from his pocket. "See this? What do you think this is?"

"It looks like a piece of gold; maybe pyrite, Uncle," Bob answered.

"Good guess; I've had this graded at a metallurgist shop in Traverse—gold flecks; found at the gravel pit down the river road near the migrant encampment. I've checked the deed with experts in Traverse. It's mine. But you and I know I've been followed, my shed behind the big house ransacked, and Aunty in a fit-to-be tied situation. I also had the clay and calcite tested. Seems I own a pit worth millions if and when I can excavate, probably next spring. And Ed Sneed was caught. All my maps, diagrams, and contraptions were returned. I put all these items in a safer bank in Traverse.

"So here we are, Bob; don't know who killed Morris Tanner . . . still an open investigation. Your friend Daniel is off the hook for now; he's no person of interest. The McChesney crew is staying mum for the time being.

"Aunty and I are packin' our bags soon and goin' south; I gotta sell those new year-round motor homes. I haven't made much money up here this past season—just breakin' even, if that.

"We'll stay in touch over the winter. I'll write. I know you can put pen to paper. Stay in touch. The whole gang will be back next spring, you bein' here next early summer—another season," he said, drifting off, his voice raspy. The cold temperatures ripped at his body. The pounding of the waves from the Big Lake, making this season uninviting, made Uncle wonder why there should be a winter season—a resort season—should ever come to fruition in this north community.

Then he pondered, the Indigenous population survived the harsh winters—so can the post war generation find escape in these blustery conditions.

"We're skipping the dump today. A last meal, Bob, before you go home. No turkey—just Aunty's creative soul makin' special pot roast plus fruit compote for dessert—and her left over bread pudding. Let's grab some grub before it's too late. I ring my own dinner bell, Bob. I hear it callin' our name."

The two made their way to the dining room where Aunty was prepared for the family. This out-of-season meal for Bob now was comforting. Uncle, Aunty, uncle's son, daughter-in-law, and a few selected guests—Cordy and Mr. and Mrs. Mack—would all enjoy this last meal before Bob would go home. He still had the rest of the school year ahead of him before the summer break.

He knew Uncle would keep in touch with him via letters. His relationship to his uncle—close and secretive at times—would surely remain intact during this off season.

Just then the Junker clan pulled up to the house. Heather got out from the truck first followed by Mr. Junker. Mrs. Junker stayed in the cab.

Hearing the pounding on the door, Uncle—pipe firmly entrenched in his teeth—hollered, "Hold your horses!"

Mr. Junker, out of breath, exclaimed, "How ya doin', Unc'? Just came to give you the word. Maybe more so to Bobby, er Bob.

"Our Janina wants to see Bob before you goes back home. She's in bad shape. Let us take him to Munson in Traverse.

"Glad we got here before he left. Where is Bob?" Mr. Junker expending his last ounce of breath.

Uncle, slightly irritated as the flame in his pipe went out, said, "Yeah, I heard the news. *Bob,*" Uncle called out, "*someone here to talk to you!* Your business close up, too? We got some hunters this fall—that's all."

Bob appeared at the door, "Oh, hi, Mr. Junker."

"Janina wants to see you. Bad news. We'll be back in a couple of hours," said Mr. Junker, talking to two people at once.

"Get your wool jacket on, Bob—there's a chill comin'," said Aunty, bringing Bob his heavy fall coat.

The Junker family and Bob took the elevator to the fourth floor where the trauma care unit was located.

"Here we are," Heather lamented, "four fifty-two."

The room was dark, curtains pulled down. An array of flowers—bouquets of all shapes and sizes—lined the perimeter of the room resting on tables, some on a dresser with pictures of the Junker family in various poses during holidays and special events. Several were photos of Janina diving or about to dive,

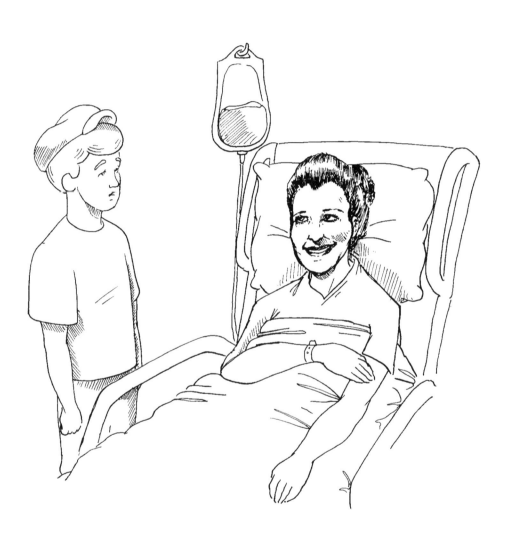

outfitted in several of her outfits some admirers referred to as costumes.

Bob caught a glimpse in one photo of her frame suspended halfway between the highest span and the emerald water below—frozen in time, back arched perfectly, arms outstretched, preserved forever—a testament to her grace and beauty.

"*Ahem*." He was startled back to reality when Mr. Junker spoke abruptly. "Over here, son. Janina is awake. You two have much to say to each other. I'll leave you alone. Come on, family, let these two have their moment."

With that comment they all departed to wait in the visitors' area.

"Over here." Janina motioned weakly with an arm that faltered abruptly. Her other arm stuck with a needle, a drip flowing into this arm hanging precariously, her weak voice almost high pitched, crying out yet modulated. Only a subdued half breathy tone reached Bob's ears.

Tears flowed from Bob's eyes. "What happened, Janina?"

"So fast. One day I was up there ready to dive, but the headaches came. The pain behind the eyes. The vomiting. I couldn't hold any food down.

"Come closer. My sight is almost gone. They've diagnosed it—a subarachnoid hemorrhage, SAH. My vessels were bulging above the aorta in the brain. In other words, brain cancer," she concluded, her eyes now closed. She appeared to be asleep, motionless.

"I'm so sorry, Janina." Bob's mind spun in several different directions. He was speechless. Looking at her now, all hooked up, heart monitor engaged, the smell of Lysol and other disinfectants in the air; the hospital setting personified caused him to want to wretch in the nearest wastebasket.

For what seemed like an hour, maybe two minutes passed. Silence between patient and visitor.

Bob noticed her face now pale, freckles not noticeable. That long black licorice hair once hanging in strands was now packaged in a bun-like mass.

Her breathing became heavy and her voice raspy. She began to speak in low tones, barely audible: "It started at the end of summer. You were gone. One day I was up high, the highest cable strand, and the headache unbearable. Funny, I thought, where is that cameo charm around Bob's neck.

"The bright speckled colors saved me from falling one time. But the headaches got worse. I dove that day—end of summer anyway—but the pain persisted behind the eye. Then the blood clotted in my brain. Doctors ran their tests. I had a four millimeter bulging vessel above the aorta in the brain. For a month or so I lost my vision.

"Finally, I was diagnosed with anaplastic oligodendroglioma grade three—a fast growing tumor. I'm due soon for radiation and chemo treatment. The good cells will be destroyed as well as the cancer. My chance of survival is less than 50-50." She now slumped back, exhausted. Her eyes closed. Though weak, she held out a hand. Bob placed his hand on hers.

Again, his thoughts raced. Why, in this moment, did she seem so calm while he was at a loss for words and out of breath himself? He thought surely this young lady—perhaps twenty years his senior, too young to die, having been operated on—would return to normal and things would be okay. Surely she would dive again. Maybe, however, this was a part of her life she would put behind her. Not too old, just at a point in her existence where she would go on to new pursuits. Let someone else do the diving. How could he think now of such a silly ritual. Every day these past few years he watched her form spiral into the rapid flowing river below.

It seemed he grew up from the child behind a clump of logs and weeds watching her, excited as a child that a full grown adult would take such a chance as to jump from a high place into a swirling, churning river below. Wasn't that young experience for him a witness to life and death. What if Janina hit an obstruction flying down. What if, by chance, a small boat snuck under the bridge, and she struck the boat below. And what if the dive itself failed and she somehow twisted her torso the wrong way, wrenched her back, did a belly smack, anything, he thought, causing the dive itself to go wrong.

Her eyelids flickered. Her faint voice, muffled, came out of hiding, "You and me. What a pair we made. What imaginary games you played from behind that brush pile. You came most days to play among the cattails and brush. Did you plan to be there when I dove that first time, or was I just some adult you grew accustomed to—jumping you might say—taking a chance not to get hurt—foolishly doing what no other of your adult guardians would do?

"Then one day, one year, I confronted you. Come out from your childish games. Confront the real world.

"But then why would I care what you did with your summers under that brush pile. Don't we all grow up and move on? I just took a special interest in what, I thought, was a young boy, learning about nature, surrounding himself with a non-human world. You the shy one, me bringing you out of your shell. But what do I know?

"Time goes by. You're growing up fast. Let me say when that intruder came into your world, my understanding was you remained calm. You talked to him calmly. No screaming or yelling. I think you said, *You need help, mister.*

"What'll happen to me Bob, I don't know. But we connected, didn't we. The diver and the boy in the brush pile. I have a 50-50 chance of survival. The tumor will probably come back. But I've had a great life up to now. You know up here in the North Woods we have all the fresh air we need to be very healthy and then some."

Her breathing now became labored. She felt sick to her stomach. Her head hurt as she felt pulsing, horrible throbbing.

"Oh, by the way, didn't I introduce you to my sister Heather? You and she are about the same age. Take good care of her. You two can be a matched pair. The pain is getting worse."

With that she hit the call button. When the nurse arrived, she politely told Bob his time was up.

Again, it seemed Janina, the sick one, defined the moment; he was the quiet one who couldn't figure out what this private time with her meant. He would go back to his aunty and uncle and say goodbye—this off season, going home to finish the school year.

He would stay in touch with the Junker family. He would look forward to coming up next summer.

What this all meant between him and Janina was a total mystery. The diver who made his early life fun but confusing; now he being older—a teen—her diving part of his machinations—

growing up still totally confusing.

And, again, in this hospital room, this time, this day, she defined the moment. He came up short on being able to explain any of his teen feelings—not able to put them into a sensible structure—tongue tied at best—completely out of touch with the real world of male-female relations at worst.

The Junkers surrounded him in the visitors' area. "Time to go back to your uncle and aunty." Heather smiled, and Bob was at a loss for words—again.

"You'll be up I'm sure next summer. Write me—we had fun at the barbecue picnic. I'm still wiping marshmallow off my mush," Heather continued her monologue.

Mr. Junker took over the conversation. "We'll wait and see how Janina improves over time as I'm sure she will. She's a fighter. Her spirit soars and her soul runs deep. The Good Lord will guide us all through these tough times.

Bob said goodbye to Aunty, Uncle, and all the guests who had gathered for this off-season Thanksgiving get-together. He would wait again for the north wind to beckon him this coming summer. He would be among friends again in this pristine world and would be captured by the Big Lake with its eternal myriad of blue coloring and haunting history.